MURDER ON
WARBLER WEEKEND

Jan Dunlap

NORTH STAR PRESS OF ST. CLOUD, INC.
St. Cloud, Minnesota

ISBN-10: 0-87839-321-8
ISBN-13: 978-0-87839-221-3

First Edition, September 1, 2009

Printed in the United States of America

Published by
North Star Press of St. Cloud, Inc.
P.O. Box 451
St. Cloud, Minnesota 56302

northstarpress.com

info@northstarpress.com

CHAPTER ONE

IT WAS THE KIND OF SPRING MORNING birders dream about.

Clear.

Sunny.

Warm.

Not a breeze ruffling the new leaves on the trees.

Warblers everywhere, singing, darting.

My mother screaming.

Okay, maybe that part wasn't exactly a birder's dream come true.

Actually, that part was more like a nightmare.

It was the second Saturday in May. Just after dawn, I'd swung by my parents' home to pick up my mom for our annual bird-watching date on the day before Mother's Day. "Birds with Bob" she calls it. "Making Mom-points," I call it. After her bugging me for years to take her birding, I finally gave in a couple years ago. To be honest, it was an act of desperation. I'd forgotten it was Mother's Day and hadn't even gotten her a card. Bad, bad son. On the spur of the moment, I suggested we go birding together, and before I knew it, she had a baseball cap on her head and my dad's binoculars around her neck.

She thought it was great.

I thought it was pathetic.

Not that my mom was pathetic—she's wonderful. It's just that when I go birding, I go for hours—heck, let's be honest, days—at a time, in remote locations all over the state of Minnesota. Mom was

1

happy with a thirty-minute walk around the nearby golf course. We saw Robins, Red-winged Blackbirds, a few Canada Geese, and four Yellow-rumped Warblers.

She was impressed.

I was embarrassed.

As one of the best birders in the state, I figured I could do a lot better than that for my own mother.

Since then, I've tried to broaden her birding horizons a little more each year. Last year, I took her on a short walk through Purgatory. That's the name of a wildlife area, not my name for the experience. Although it might just as well have been, since it rained the whole hour we were there. It was cold, too, and I think we only got about eight species where I normally find at least twenty. Then on the way back to the car, Mom stepped into a mud hole that sucked off her shoe. Of course, it was her favorite old shoe, and I practically had to restrain her from diving into the mud after it.

"I'll buy you another pair," I told her, having to shout over the sound of the pouring rain.

"It won't be the same," she shouted back. "I loved that shoe. I wore that shoe to all your baseball games, Bob."

"Mom, that was twenty years ago." I opened the car door and helped her up. Mom's just five feet tall, and it's a big step up for her into my SUV. I ran around the front end and hopped into the driver's seat.

She squinted at me. "No. Twenty years? It can't be. I look at you, and I still see my chubby-cheeked baby boy." She patted my cheeks, which were covered with rain and a week's worth of new beard. That didn't seem to register with Mom.

"You're so cute," she said.

"You're so sappy," I replied.

"Smartass," she laughed. "Now take me home. I need to get the mud out from between my toes."

So, as you might imagine, I was thrilled to see clear skies on this morning because the last thing I wanted was a repeat of Purgatory.

This year, I wanted to give my mom a "Birds with Bob" she'd boast about. One she could remember fondly with great regard for my extraordinarily amazing birding skills. For that, there was only one place to go: Murphy-Hanrehan Regional Park. Located south of the Minnesota River, it's one of the premiere Twin Cities spots for catching warblers in spring migration, and since I'd already been out there myself the previous weekend, scoping out the birding, I knew it would be a winner of a day. Not only was the weather perfect, but the foliage on the trees was still new, big enough to give the birds adequate protection, but not so big that it completely screened them from our view. On top of that, our late cool spring had held up migration, resulting in tons of birds hanging around the area later than they usually did.

"This is going to be great," I assured her as we climbed out of my Cardinal-red SUV at the trailhead parking area. "I bet we see at least two dozen species in the next hour."

"You think so?" she asked. She slathered some sunscreen on her cheeks and offered me the bottle. "That would be good, right?"

She rubbed the lotion into her skin, remembering to get both the back of her neck and her throat. I'd reminded her earlier about "warbler neck," the stiffness one gets from holding one's head straight back to try to see the birds in the tops of the trees. Yes, it's true: birding can be a literal pain in the neck. Sometimes it's a pain in the ass, too—those nine-hour round-trip drives I occasionally make to northwestern Minnesota to put a new bird on my life list leave me car-seat-sore for days. Today, though, I was making sure my mom was the well-prepared birder. I didn't want her red-throated and sore-necked for Mother's Day. She handed me the bottle, and I squeezed some sunscreen out for myself.

"You know, I'd love to have a great birding story to tell tomorrow night when everyone's over for dinner," she added, turning her face towards the bright morning sun and soaking in the warmth. "Hey, this birding thing isn't too bad when the sun's out. I like this a lot more than last year already."

So did I. Dry was definitely an improvement. Sun was even better.

I handed the bottle back to her. "We'll see what we can do, Mom. Maybe we'll luck out and find a rarity—a bird that doesn't normally show up here."

"A rarity," she repeated, stuffing her water bottle into her jacket pocket. "That sounds good. Lead the way, Bob."

We started out on the path that skirted the lake and turned into the woods. A hard rain the night before had left everything freshly washed, making all the leaves and mosses sparkle with tiny diamonds in the morning sun. The earth smelled ripe, mixed with the thick, rich scent of lilacs and wild cherry blossoms. And just as I had predicted, the warblers were bountiful. Actually, more than bountiful. Two hundred feet from the car and they were thick as flies.

"Geez Louise," Mom said, her binos in her hands. "I don't even need to use the glasses to see these guys. It's like they're swarming or something."

What they were doing was feeding on the insects that had just hatched in the last few days. Thanks to the cold spring, the birds hadn't had enough food sources to keep moving north. Now they were feasting and, in the process, giving Mom and me better views of warblers than I'd seen in years. In less than an hour, we saw literally hundreds of Yellow-rumped Warblers, Tennessee Warblers, Yellow Warblers, Black-and-white Warblers, several Orange-crowned Warblers, Common Yellowthroats, and a few Blue-winged Warblers. As is always the case with migration, we also got a lot of other birds mixed in with the warblers: an Eastern Wood-Pewee, a Brown Thrasher, a Great Crested Flycatcher, and Yellow-throated and Red-eyed Vireos. Along the trail we were walking, a handful of Scarlet Tanagers practically buzzed us, flitting back and forth, perching in the branches as we passed, then zipping back and then ahead of us again. A few times they flew so close to my head, I could have almost reached out and grabbed one.

I stopped walking and told Mom to listen.

All around us, birds were vocalizing.

"Music," Mom said. "Who's singing, Bob?"

I began to rattle off the names of the birds as I identified each species by ear. "Magnolia Warbler. Nashville Warbler. American Redstart. Blue-winged Warbler. That's the *beee* sound, followed by a lower note *bzzz*. And there's a Hermit Thrush," I said, pointing at three o'clock as we crossed the old boardwalk over the marsh. "I don't see him, but I sure hear him. And that *vreeep, vreeep,* that's the Great Crested Flycatcher."

"Forget music," Mom said. "This is a whole symphony."

And then she started screaming.

Talk about a discordant note.

For the briefest moment, I thought she was trying to add to the chorus, but I'd never thought her that tone deaf. Then I turned around and saw her standing back on the boardwalk, near the edge of the old weathered planks. She wasn't looking up into the trees where the warblers were, but staring down into the water and yelling her head off. The marsh grasses were just starting to send up bright green shoots, so the water was still fairly open and clear, not tangled with vegetation like it would be in another few months.

What was she looking at? Water snakes?

Mom had never been crazy about snakes, but these would have to be giant anacondas for her to be screaming like that, and I was pretty sure anacondas don't migrate north to Minnesota with the warblers. At least, they hadn't so far.

I ran up next to her and followed her gaze down.

Yup. No snakes. That was the good news.

A body that was there, though—that was the bad news.

"Holy shit," I said, instinctively backing away. I grabbed my mom and pulled her back, too.

Even from several feet away, I couldn't take my eyes off the body —a woman—floating just under the surface of the water. The face was bloated and pearly white. Remembrances of the Death Marshes scene from *Lord of the Rings* hit me hard. Hair drifted around her head like

a clump of tangled milfoil. A soft thumping noise reverberated along the planks under our feet, and I guessed that the rest of the body was lodged beneath the boardwalk, apparently trapped between the supporting piles driven into the marsh bottom.

Talk about a rare sighting.

"Hey, Mom, it's Mother's Day. How about I take you to see the first warblers of the season? And maybe a dead body, too?"

I shook my head in utter disbelief. This was worse than Purgatory. This was Hell. Although, if nothing else, my mom sure had her birding tale to tell at dinner because I was pretty damn sure no one could top this one.

Unfortunately.

Thankfully.

I took my mom's arm and practically dragged her off the boardwalk onto dry land. She'd quit screaming, but now was hyperventilating and shaking all over. I wrapped my arms around her and held tight.

"Mom, it's okay," I whispered, rocking her back and forth and patting her on the back until she was breathing a little more normally again. It reminded me of all the times she'd held me when I was a little kid, rocking me, patting my back, making everything all right again. Moms do that. Moms fix things. Although, let's face it, my mom never had to make a dead body all right again, either, so I definitely had the shorter end of the stick here. "It's okay, Mom," I repeated.

"No, it's not," she muttered into the front of my jacket. "I think I'm going to throw up." She pushed away from me and lost it at the side of the trail. I stood behind her, feeling a little sick myself.

Gee, wasn't this fun? Not just a waterlogged corpse, but nausea, too. Way better than pouring rain and shoe-sucking mud. What a great way to start the weekend. Yup, this was really going to be a special Mother's Day this year. Forget the cards and flowers. Bond with Mom over nausea.

"Move over," I told her.

I bent next to my mom and put my hands on my knees. I took a few deep breaths and the nausea passed. My mom, meanwhile, had

rinsed her mouth out with some of her bottled water and spit it out into the grass.

"I don't know, Bob," she said. "Maybe I'm just not cut out for birding. Maybe I should take up stamp collecting instead. You know. Inside. Alone. No bodies."

No kidding. Seeing a body in the water, mere months after finding one frozen in the Northwoods, even had me thinking twice about birding, and I'd been birding since I was eight years old.

"I need your cell phone, Mom."

I noticed that her hands were a little shaky, but she managed to pull the phone out of her windbreaker pocket and hand it to me. I dialed 911.

After I finished talking with the dispatcher, I took Mom a little farther away from the marsh. We found a bench next to the trail and sat down to wait for the police. Neither of us said anything for a couple minutes. Then my mom heaved a big sigh and looked up at the cloudless blue sky. Two mallards flew overheard. "This really sucks," she said.

"Well, yeah," I agreed. "I don't suppose 'Happy Mother's Day, Mom' would help at the moment, would it?"

She turned her head to look at me. "I hope this isn't like some weird family curse." I could see tears starting to well in her eyes.

It occurred to me that maybe I should make her lie down. I mean, she was no spring chicken anymore, and maybe she was getting a delayed reaction. She had found a dead body, for crying out loud. It wasn't something on her usual Saturday morning "to-do" list. Do laundry. Thaw roast. Find corpse. I stared at her pupils, but they looked okay.

"What are you doing?" she asked me.

"Checking your pupils. You know, for shock." Actually, that's something I'm really good at. I aced that portion of my Red Cross training when I was in grad school getting my counseling degree. Anytime you think you might be going into shock, just let me know. One look and I can tell.

"I'm not going into shock," Mom said. "I was talking about find-ing dead people. First you find that body up north a couple months ago while you were looking for that Boreal Owl, and now I find a body here. If your father finds a body, I'm going into therapy." She seemed to be thinking it over. "And what about Lily? If she found a body, she'd fall apart. Poor Lily."

"Mom, Lily's not going to find a body," I assured her. "I don't think this is something you need to worry about."

But—I could have added, but didn't—if Lily did, I'd be more worried about the corpse than Lily. My sister might look like a shrimp—she's a foot shorter than my six-foot-three—but she's tough. She runs her own business and takes no prisoners. She's a rabid fan of the Minnesota Wild hockey team, with the operative word being "rabid." She's also into kick-boxing, so I wouldn't suggest trying to sneak up on her in a dark alley, either. On top of that, she's really skilled with gardening implements and not afraid to use them. I'd never, ever, call Lily "poor anything" as long as I liked breathing.

In the distance, finally, I heard a siren wailing. A few minutes later, the police were coming down the trail on the other side of the marsh. I put my hand under my mom's elbow and helped her stand up. We walked back to where the boardwalk started, but neither of us wanted to step on the planks again. A knot of officers and emergency personnel were already assessing the scene, crouching at the edge of the boards, taking pictures and preparing to remove the body. A big man in a sheriff's uni-form left the group and crossed the rest of the walk to meet us.

"I'm Sheriff Kowiak," he said, shaking my mother's hand and then mine. "Looks like you've had quite a morning, here. I assume you're the folks who called this in." He nodded back to the cluster of people on the boardwalk.

"Bob White," I said, introducing myself. "I'm the one who called. This is my mother, Evelyn White. She . . . ah . . . found the body."

Somehow, that just wasn't something I'd ever imagined on a list of things to say about my mother. Makes great brownies, yes. Worries too

much, naturally. Finds corpses? I don't think so. And isn't there some nicer way to say it? Like, maybe, "She found a previously alive person?"

"We're going to have to have you stick around for a while," Kowiak said. "I need to ask you some questions."

Having just done the drill two months ago in connection with the owl murder, I had a pretty good idea how the next hour would go and what to expect. Mom and I would recite our movements since arriving in the park at six-thirty this morning. We'd provide our personal information. We'd answer questions. We'd repeat the same stuff to three or four officers. We'd buy tickets to the upcoming policemen's barbecue.

What I didn't expect, however, was what the sheriff said when we were finally getting ready to walk back to my car parked at the trailhead.

"Mr. White, I'd appreciate it if you wouldn't tell the family before I can speak with them."

I looked at him, surprised. What family? I had no idea who the dead woman was. How would I know the family?

He read my puzzled expression and frowned. "I figured you knew the deceased, seeing as you're a counselor at Savage High School."

Okay, so that was interesting. "It's a big school," I said. "I don't know all the students, let alone their parents." The teachers I knew, and Face in the Water wasn't any one of those.

So, now that he'd indicated it was a parent from Savage, I couldn't walk away without knowing who had drowned in Murphy-Hanrehan's Marsh.

"Who is it?" I asked, afraid to hear the answer.

"Nancy Olson," Kowiak said. "Did you know her?"

The bottom fell out of my stomach. For a second, I couldn't get my breath to answer. "No," I finally managed to say. "I never met her."

Amazing. Even over the roaring sound in my ears, I could still hear hundreds of warblers singing in the trees. "But I counsel her daughter almost every day."

CHAPTER TWO

Oh, man, Bob. Not Dani Olson's mom."

I had just finished telling my good buddy Alan Thunderhawk about my morning excursion and its deadly finale. We were sitting out on the deck of my town house, both of us shirtless, drinking a beer and enjoying the feel of the warm afternoon sunshine on our Minnesota hides. Even though I'd coated my face and neck in lotion, I knew I'd pay later with a sunburn for the pleasure of exposing my chest and shoulders, but the heat on my skin was too good to miss after another long winter. It was just one of the curses I endured for being red-headed and fair-skinned. Alan, of course, being Lakota, would just look manfully bronzed by nightfall. By Monday, I knew he'd be rubbing it in, calling me "Red-man" instead of the usual "White-man" he'd christened me when we roomed together in college.

The only thing I'd be rubbing in was the sunburn cream.

"She's a great kid," Alan was saying. "And she tries so hard. Given her family situation, it's amazing she does as well as she does. And now this? How much can the kid take? What with her parents and all."

"I hope this doesn't crack her. The poor kid can't catch a break."

"Do you think she'll be in school on Monday?" Alan asked.

"No idea," I answered. "I can certainly understand she might not be able to deal with school so soon, but then again, maybe being with her friends in some semblance of a normal routine will hold her up."

I looked out at the woods behind my house and took another swallow of beer. Brightly colored American Goldfinches swept through the tree branches and Red-chested House Finches sat on all the perches of the bird feeder attached to my deck's corner post. Earlier in the day, I'd seen a Baltimore Oriole feeding on the grape jelly I'd left on the hummingbird feeder. Northern Cardinals and Bluejays had put in multiple appearances throughout the day, and last night, I'd listened to the calls of the Great Horned Owl that nested in the woods. The backyard was one of the reasons I'd bought this town house. It was a haven for both me and the birds.

I looked back at Alan. "She told me that school was about the only place she really felt safe."

Alan shook his head. "Man, sometimes I just want to smack these parents. Don't they even have a clue to the damage they do to their kids? Sometimes I think the cases of physical abuse are the easier ones—at least that way, the damage is visible, and we can get some social services involved, or move the kid out of the house and start dealing with it."

He rubbed his beer can across his chin and his voice went soft. "But the kids who suffer on the inside, the ones like Dani—those kids are the ones who really tear me apart. They're doing everything they can possibly do to keep afloat, but what they really need is just for their parents to parent."

I tipped my beer in his direction. "You're preaching to the choir, Alan."

Unfortunately, as a counselor, I saw it all the time. There were plenty of dysfunctional families around, and they came in all shapes, sizes, colors, and socio-economic classes. Over the years, I'd known students who paid the household bills because their parents forgot, or just didn't care. I knew other students who had asked neighbors to get up after midnight and drive them down to the county jail so they could bail their parents out of the drunk tank. When I thought about how many students still managed to finish high school despite awful family circumstances, I was always stunned. Grateful, but stunned.

Truth be told, Dani's situation wasn't the worst I'd seen, but still bad enough. Her dad spent almost every night at Little Six, one of several casinos within a twenty-mile radius of Savage. When he rolled in at about two in the morning, she'd wake up to the sound of her mom screaming at him, threatening to leave him, or have him jailed for stealing from her to finance another night at the blackjack table. Most nights, Dani told me, she didn't get back to sleep before she had to get up for school at six o'clock. After school, she worked a part-time job till early evening. By the time she got home to fix herself a late supper, her dad was already gone, and her mom was brooding and unapproachable, at best.

At worst, she yelled at Dani for her every move.

And that was just the part Dani was willing to tell me about. I wondered if there was more she wasn't willing to share.

"She tells me I'm stupid," Dani had told me one day, crying. "She yells at me that I'm lazy and she's ashamed to have me for a daughter. If it weren't for my brother, I'd run away, Mr. White. He's the only one who cares about me. He tells me just to ignore Mom, that she's the one who's stupid."

Dani had calmed down then and wiped her eyes and wet cheeks. "But he says he's working on something for both of us, so I won't have to run away." She'd balled up the tissue she'd been holding and tried to smile. "He says I'll be able to come live with him, and I won't have to deal with my mom anymore."

I'd heard that one before. In cases like Dani's, there always seemed to be a friend or cousin somewhere who was going to come riding to the rescue of the student trapped in an impossible position. In reality, though, it rarely happened; the risks for the friend or cousin turned out to be too great, the legal system's hands too tied by miles of red tape, or at the last minute, the student herself just couldn't walk away. Again and again, I saw the truth that the bonds of blood were almost impossible to sever, even when they were choking the life out of the individuals involved.

But now, Dani's mom was dead. What would that mean for Dani? Would she be able to pull herself together, move on, get a fresh start, or would her already tenuous world crumble into even smaller pieces?

Awfully sobering thoughts for a sunny afternoon.

"So," I said to Alan, making a deliberate effort to completely change the subject, "how's the school's newest environmental radical coming along in his plans to form a citizen's action group on his way to taking over the world?"

Alan tossed his empty beer can in a perfect arc to land in the recycling container sitting out on my deck. "The boy's a natural, White-man. He's got charm, charisma, intelligence, drive, and this community-service mindset that won't quit. Don't know that I'd call him a radical, though. Karl's savvy enough to know he'll catch more flies with honey than a flyswatter."

Karl Solvang is one of my shining stars at Savage. A senior, he was all set to go to George Washington University next fall, majoring in political science.

He was also the only person I've ever met who actually planned to become the president of the United States.

Really.

He was planning to be the President of the United States.

When he'd come to me a few weeks ago looking for help in organizing a citizen's group to oppose a proposed entertainment complex development near his grandparents' farm, I'd sent him to Alan. Since Alan had done a stint as a community organizer before he'd earned his doctorate in political science and turned up at Savage as a teacher, I figured he could give Karl some pointers on community activism. As it turned out, the two had really hit it off. Now Alan was doing some serious mentoring with Karl, teaching him a lot about the political process and grassroots organization.

"We've got a potluck tomorrow night," Alan said. "Karl's got about twenty-five people coming to a picnic right in the middle of the acreage of the proposed development. In fact," he said, taking off his old cowboy hat to swipe his wrist across his sweaty forehead, "you might want to be there. One of the agenda items is planning a bird survey one night next week to evaluate the extent of the bird population on the acreage and how it might be impacted by high noise levels."

"Really? I might have to put in an appearance, then. Promise me birds *and* Tater Tot hotdish, and I'll be there."

"Hotdish, huh? Okay, I'll bring one myself," Alan offered.

"Oh. In that case, forget it."

He swung his hat at my head, but I leaned out of the way.

"If there's birding, I'll be there," I assured him. "You know that."

Besides which, I had an ulterior motive: I'd decided to try and find every warbler in migration. That meant that along with all the usual suspects, I'd have to track down a Kentucky Warbler and a Yellow-breasted Chat, the two most elusive of all the warblers.

It had been a few years since I'd seen either of them—thanks to increasing commercial and residential developments in the areas they liked to frequent, their sightings were getting more rare all the time. The last time I'd seen a Chat, in fact, it hadn't been far from the acreage that Karl was interested in preserving. Maybe if I went to the picnic, I'd get lucky and get them both—a plate of Tater Tot hotdish and a Chat.

But then I remembered that tomorrow night was already booked.

"Can't do it," I told Alan. "Luce and I are having Sunday dinner with Mom and Dad for Mother's Day. But count me in for the bird survey next week. And if you need a few more birders, let me know. I'm sure I can flush a few out of the bushes to lend a hand."

That was probably a gross understatement on my part. A few phone calls, and there'd be birders hanging out of the trees all over that property. If I was remembering correctly, the acreage of Karl's crusade was adjacent to Louisville Swamp, another one of my favorite spots for birding during warbler migration. If the proposed development went through, it would certainly mean loss of habitat and a negative impact on the avian population in the swamp, which would mean bad news for birders like me. For years, it had been the only place in the whole Twin Cities metropolitan area where I could find a Prothonotary Warbler, and the few times I've gotten a Louisiana Waterthrush, it was at Louisville. From a totally selfish perspective, I needed the swamp intact and undisturbed to provide me with the birds this year, too. Before my mom had discovered Dani's mother in the marsh this morning, I'd been feeling good about my chances of finding every warbler. Now, recalling all the spring seasons that the Chat had been invisible and silent, I wasn't so confident.

But birders are nothing if not eternal optimists. I'd do the survey with Karl's group and see what I could find.

"So, how is the lovely Luce?" Alan was saying.

I thought about my girlfriend and smiled.

"Good," I said. "She still thinks you're too short for her, by the way."

Alan laughed. "By a lousy two inches. I'm telling you, Bob, you better marry that woman. She's about as perfect as you're going to find."

"Yeah, I know. She birds, she cooks, she loves me. What more could I ask?"

Alan shook his head and looked me in the eye. "You could ask her to marry you."

I looked him right back in the eye. "I already did," I said.

For a moment, Alan froze. Then he opened his mouth, closed it, opened it and closed it again. Very basslike. I wondered if he could do a walleye.

"You proposed to her?" he finally managed to choke out.

"Yeah, sort of," I hedged.

He narrowed his eyes. "What is 'sort of'?"

Now I was doing the fish imitation. I'd opened my big fat mouth, and Alan had slipped the hook right in. Unfortunately for me, "catch and release" wasn't a part of his vocabulary.

I shifted in my lounge chair. "We were up north, and we were watching some ducks in the water, and I got to thinking how ducks mate for life, and that if anyone was watching Luce and me, we probably looked like a mated pair—you know—we're both tall and slim and we were birding together—and it just popped out."

Alan continued staring at me, his expression slipping toward pity. Then he burst out laughing. "You proposed to Luce because you were looking at ducks? What did you say, 'Marry me, quack-quack?' 'Let's build a nest together?' Oh, my God, I'm gonna die here."

I watched him laugh so hard he fell off his chair.

"Okay, so maybe it wasn't the most romantic moment I could have imagined. What is the big deal, Alan?" I asked, trying not to let my growing irritation show. Like he was any expert in the proposal department. "You're the one who's always telling me I should ask her. You were just saying it again, for cripe's sake."

"Hey," he said, spreading his arms wide and still laughing. "That's great. I mean, that's great! I just can't believe you finally did it. About time, too. Definitely a good thing. Congratulations, Whiteman! Have you set a date?"

"Well," I said, feeling like I needed to do a little back-peddling. "It's not really official. I mean,"—I hesitated—"she didn't say yes, exactly."

"What is not saying yes 'exactly'?" Alan asked, his eyes tight on my face.

What she'd said was "Eventually." At the time, I'd been partly relieved and partly disappointed. Now that I was thinking about it again, however, that "eventually" was starting to bother me. After all, I hadn't asked her if she wanted to marry me specifically. It was more a general question about her interest in getting married at some point.

I had just assumed she was referring to me.

And you know what they say about making assumptions—it makes an "ass" out of "u" and "me." Maybe I should reopen this conversation with her, I realized. At thirty-four, neither of us was getting

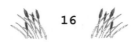

any younger. Maybe two years of dating was enough. Maybe it was time to make a change, a commitment. I was pretty sure, given enough time, I could think of a better way to propose than by watching ducks.

At least, I hoped I could.

"Long story," I sighed. I finished my beer, tossed it in the recycling bin, then turned and punched Alan in the shoulder. "I have an idea. Let's talk about *your* love life. Who's the woman of the week, oh, mighty Hawk?"

But before he could answer, my doorbell started ringing.

"You get a reprieve, buddy. I'll be right back." I got up, slid open the deck doors and headed through the living room to the front hall. With the windows open, I could hear my backyard birds singing throughout the whole house. I loved that. Without even thinking about it, I was naming off the birds in my head. I opened the front door.

"I think I might have gotten you into trouble, Mr. White."

Fifteen-year-old Dani Olson was on my front step. Her face was blotchy from crying.

"I told the police I was here last night. Sleeping with you."

CHAPTER THREE

"S ay again?"

Dani shifted on her feet, staring at the ground and refusing to make eye contact with me. "The police asked me where I was last night, and I told them I was here with you. Sleeping. All night."

Yup, that's what I thought she said the first time. Holy crap. I was going to learn how to make license plates.

"Ah, Bob, maybe you should bring her inside," Alan suggested from somewhere behind me. He'd obviously followed me into the house from the deck and heard what Dani had said.

"Yeah, right," I said, snapping out of my momentary paralysis. I pulled Dani into the house and shut the door behind her. Guess we didn't need the whole neighborhood hearing about my seducing a minor. Crap! Said minor was now *inside* my house. What was I thinking? I reached past her to reopen the door and was about to push her back outside, but Alan caught my arm.

"Bob, it's okay. Let me talk to her. Go put on a shirt," he said, his voice amazingly calm and in control. Which probably good because I was close to wetting my pants. "And bring me one, too, while you're at it."

Dani's head snapped up. Her eyes went wide as she took in our bare chests. "Are you guys gay?"

Oh, great. Now I had a choice: rumors that I was sleeping with a student or rumors that Alan and I were gay.

"Is that why you guys aren't married?"

I rolled my eyes and went to retrieve our shirts from the deck. By the time I got back, Dani was sitting on the sofa in my living room, talking quietly with Alan.

"I'm afraid to go home, Mr. Thunderhawk," Dani sniffled. "The police were there all morning, and my dad was getting so angry, I could tell."

I handed Alan his t-shirt and gave Dani my sternest look.

"And that was why you told the police you were sleeping with me? Dani, do you have any idea what you've done?"

She burst into wails.

"Smooth move, counselor," Alan observed. "The kid's barely coherent, her mother's dead, she's afraid of her father, and she's got nowhere to go. Have you got any tissues?"

Of course I had tissues. "Tissues" was my middle name. I was a high school counselor. I always had students crying around me. Heck, I should put it on my vanity license plate—the one I was going to make while I served time in prison for supposedly sleeping with a fifteen-year-old student. Or maybe I should just go with JAILBIRD on the plate. That had a nice ring to it. Not that I'd be driving anywhere for, say, the next twenty years or so. Good thing my life list of birds was already a long one because I sure wasn't going to be adding much to it in the foreseeable future.

"Bob," Alan said. "Tissues."

I stalked into the kitchen, tore a handful from the box there and returned to the living room. "Here," I told Dani, laying them on her lap.

Get a grip, I told myself. *This kid needs all the help she can get and she came to you for it.*

"Dani," I started over. "I'm so sorry about your mom. I know things were strained between you, but this . . . I'm sorry."

She wiped her cheeks and eyes with the tissues, then looked up at me. "I didn't mean to get you in trouble, Mr. White. I just didn't

know what to say anymore, and I thought they'd stop asking me questions if I told them I wasn't there. I thought if they thought I was with an adult, it would be okay. I didn't mean the sex thing. Really."

I nodded. "Yeah. We'll get it straightened out."

"But you've got to tell the police the truth, Dani," Alan reminded her. "It's the only way they can do their job. Where were you last night if you weren't at home?"

Dani's eyes locked onto the floor again. "At Mandy's."

Dani, Mandy Walters, and Alicia Notermann were a tight threesome, I knew. It was also a rare event when I didn't see at least two of them in my office on any given day. Fortunately, the reasons for their visits were usually minor infractions of school rules; tardiness and "personal issues" were the typical complaints. "So why didn't you tell the police that?" I asked. "Why bring me into it?"

"Mandy's mom and dad were gone for the night, Mr. White. There weren't any adults there." She still wouldn't make eye contact with me as she twisted the tissue in her hands. "I didn't want Mandy or her parents to get in trouble because of me."

So what do I look like? I wondered. *A male model for orange jumpsuits?*

"I'm sorry, Mr. White," Dani said again. "Really. I didn't mean to get you in trouble."

I took a little measure of encouragement that the vice squad hadn't shown up at my door yet. Maybe I wasn't going to learn license plate manufacturing as a second career after all. In fact, now that I could think more clearly about it, I expected the police had a lot of experience in dealing with teenagers and their sometimes skewed versions of reality, especially during times when they were under duress. Dani's mom had been found dead in a marsh; if that wasn't duress, I didn't know what was.

"Dani, Mr. Thunderhawk and I are going to take you home now." Since there was no way I was taking Dani anywhere without at least one other adult in the car, Alan had just been appointed official chaperone.

If I'd had my druthers, a whole crowd would have been nice, but Alan, being available, would have to do. "Is there anyone who could come and stay with you there?" I asked Dani. "I know you're afraid of your dad right now."

"I'll call my brother," she said. "Now that my mom's . . . not there . . . he'll come and stay with me."

"Where's he living now, Dani?" Alan asked. I vaguely remembered that Alan had had Chris in class several years back. Had the family been a mess back then, too?

"He has a trailer," she replied. "Right near the park. Not that far from our house, really."

I pulled out my car keys. "Murphy-Hanrehan?"

"Yeah, that's it."

It suddenly occurred to me that Dani probably didn't know that my mom and I were the ones who discovered her mother's body this morning.

"Dani, I need to tell you something." I threw a glance at Alan and he nodded. "My mother and I were out birding early today and we . . . we were the ones who found your mom. In the park, Dani."

Big tears formed in her eyes and ran down her cheeks. I could see her jaw muscles working, trying to hold back the sobs. She wiped the wetness off her cheeks and looked me straight in the eye.

"Chris didn't kill her, Mr. White, if that's what you're thinking. Someone else did. Can I go home now?"

AN HOUR LATER, Alan and I were back on my deck, having taken Dani home. Her dad hadn't been in the house, but Dani seemed fine with waiting there alone for her brother to show up. She promised to call the police and set them straight on her whereabouts last night, and since there were no detectives with handcuffs camped out on my front step, I figured I might still have a long career in high school counseling ahead of me. Thank goodness. With my red head, prison orange was not my best color.

"You know, dealing with a suicide is one thing, but murder is a whole different ball game, White-man," Alan pointed out. "As you know," he added.

Yeah, I did know, unfortunately. Murder complicated things. Instead of the story ending with one person's incredibly sad decision to commit suicide, which was bad enough in itself, murder opened up a very nasty and messy can of worms that seemed to spill over into all kinds of unexpected places. Dani was already defending her brother and afraid of her father—not exactly a scenario that engendered faith in the family's ability to weather this crisis together. At the same time, Dani had lied to the police, making her suspect as any kind of reliable witness or source of information about what was really going on within the Olson household. Uncovering the truth behind Nancy Olson's murder wasn't going to be pretty, and I was unspeakably grateful it wasn't my responsibility.

A Rose-breasted Grosbeak flew in to take some sunflower seeds from the feeder hanging off my deck. His colors were bright in the late day sunshine, and his rose-colored bib reminded me of warning my mom this morning about getting a sunburn on her throat from looking up in the treetops for warblers. I remembered how perfect the morning had been for birding.

It was just that everything that came after that was so lousy.

Alan and I sat in the silence for a while, finishing another beer. A female Grosbeak took the male's place at the feeder, and I wondered where their nest was.

"I was just thinking," Alan said, stretching his long arms over his head. "The county council has to vote on that development project next week."

"So?"

"It's a hot potato. A very expensive hot potato." Alan crossed his arms over his chest and gave me a calculating look. "A hot potato with a lot of money to be made—or lost—by some people. From what I've observed helping Karl out, nobody on the council wants to be seen holding that particular potato, but nobody on the council wants to throw it out, either."

I waited for him to make his point.

"Except for one person."

I had the distinct sensation of hairs rising on the back of my neck. "I don't want to know this, do I?" I asked him.

Alan leaned forward in his chair and planted his elbows on his knees. "Probably not."

He looked out over my peaceful, sun-drenched yard.

"The only person who wanted that potato permanently shredded and stuffed down the disposal was the newest bird lover on the block: Councilwoman Nancy Olson." He turned back to give me another pointed look. "The now-deceased Councilwoman Nancy Olson."

CHAPTER FOUR

I was still turning over in my head what Alan had said about Nancy Olson and the county council when Luce and I pulled into my parents' driveway on Sunday evening.

"Is Lily coming for dinner, too?" Luce asked, bringing my morbid reflections to an abrupt halt. I turned off the car motor and shifted my mental gears. After all, I had better things to occupy my time tonight. I was having Mother's Day dinner with my parents. Steaks to eat. Potato salad to pass.

Climbing out of the car, I glanced over at Luce.

I also had much nicer things I could be thinking about. Like the gorgeous woman who was waiting for me on the other side of the car. Even after almost two years, I still had to pinch myself sometimes when I looked at her. I mean, who would have thought that the gawky, too tall kid would end up with the gorgeous babe?

Sorry. I meant "woman," not "babe." Heaven forbid I say something as demeaning as "babe." I'm a counselor. I'm sensitive. I don't say things like that. It's against my professional code of ethics, as well as on my personal list of Really Stupid Things to Say. Calling any woman "babe" is right up there with offering a state trooper a doughnut when he pulls me over for speeding.

Which I only did once.

Offer a doughnut to a policeman, I mean. Now I know better. Now I offer coffee.

"I expect so," I told her, taking her hand as we walked up to my parents' front door. "She'll probably be by later. Business is crazy at Lily's Landscaping on Mother's Day. All those last minute rosebushes for moms, you know."

"Well, I hope she isn't running too late. I want to hear how her lunch with Eric Stodegard went," Luce said as I held the door for her.

"Who?" I asked.

Luce gave me that look that said I was joking and of course I knew who Eric Stodegard was.

Okay, so I was obviously out of the loop here. I had no idea who Eric Stodegard was, nor did I know that he had lunched with Lily.

So shoot me.

On second thought, let me rephrase that.

Luce, however, knew all about it, and she most definitely did care. And that's when it dawned on me that I hadn't realized that Luce and Lily had become friends, that they talked with each other when I wasn't around.

"I didn't know you guys . . . communicated," I said, stepping into the front hallway.

Luce squeezed my hand. "You know, for someone who's as sensitive as you, you can be totally oblivious sometimes. Of course, we communicate. Lily's my friend. We have a lot in common. Besides you."

Somehow, I wouldn't have connected them as a pair. Lily is headstrong, independent and bossy. Luce is independent and laid-back, like me, although I know she intimidates some of the kitchen staff she works with at the restaurant. Then again, who wouldn't be intimidated by a very tall woman who was adept in the use of very sharp knives? If I were a side of beef, I know I'd be scared.

"All right. I'll bite. Who's Eric?" I asked, glancing into the empty living room and turning towards the kitchen. I could hear my parents' voices coming in through the back patio doors, so I led Luce past the oven and refrigerator and outside into the yard. "Just don't tell me it's someone I know. I hate it when she dates someone I know. I always have to pick up the pieces she leaves behind, and somehow I always end up feeling like the guilty one."

"You make it sound like she tears men apart, Bobby. She's not a carnivore."

"Could have fooled me."

"Lily's a charming woman. She's smart, funny. Any man would be lucky to have her. But," she added, "this was a business lunch."

I guess I still looked clueless because Luce finally answered my question. "Eric is the realtor who's really pushing to get that entertainment complex built down by the swamp. He's looking for bids from area businesses to put together a whole package for developing the property. He wanted to talk to Lily about landscaping."

She looked at me almost apologetically, since she knew how I felt about the proposed development and its negative impact on the surrounding wildlife areas. "It would be a huge contract for her, Bobby."

"Bob! Luce!"

My mom was hugging Luce and giving me a kiss on the cheek. My dad was right behind her, kissing Luce on the cheek and clapping a big hand on my shoulder. I winced.

"Sunburn," I said, before he could ask.

"The bane of the Whites," Lily announced, walking through the kitchen door and joining us in the backyard. "That, and finding dead bodies, apparently."

"Gee, shrimp, thanks for reminding us," I said. I gave her my sternest look—the one that always shuts down the drama queens at school. "I was kind of hoping we could overlook that little debacle for the evening. You know, be pleasant and talk about nice things."

"You know me, Bobby—Ms. Painfully Honest."

"Make that Ms. Painfully Tactless," I suggested. "Or better yet, how about just Ms. Pain in the—"

"Okay, you two," my mom said, "no fighting. It's Mother's Day, and I want to enjoy my kids." She turned to me and patted my arm. "Bob, it's okay about yesterday. Really. I don't mind talking about it."

"Mind?" my dad snorted, laying steaks on the grill. "That's *all* she wants to talk about."

A sudden wave of guilt washed over me. Of course, my mom wanted to talk about it. She'd been through a traumatic experience. She needed support, too. She may have kept all the bases covered for me when I was growing up, but she was, after all, human. Good. Now I was feeling even worse about yesterday morning. Not only had I been negligent, but an idiot as well.

"Well, sure, I want to talk about it," Mom agreed.

Instead of being upset, though, she was animated. "Wouldn't you? I mean, really, how often does something like this happen to someone?"

"At least twice, if Bobby's your standard," Lily said.

I threw her another nasty look.

"Oh, come on, Bobby," she said. "It's not like it's a stigma or anything. It just happened. It's not like you planned it . . . did you?"

"Yeah, I really want to find corpses when I go birding. It's so boring when all I find are birds."

Lily shrugged. "Some people are accident-prone. I guess you're finding-bodies-prone."

"Actually," my mom interrupted, handing Lily the silverware to set on the picnic table, "I'm the one who found the body. Bob was already off the boardwalk, ahead of me. I saw it first."

"Could we talk about something else?" I asked.

Luce, God bless her, jumped in. "Lily, how was lunch with Eric Stodegard?"

Almost immediately, Lily's cheeks flamed pink—a sure sign she was excited, and there were only two things, to my knowledge, that excited Lily: financial profit and season tickets to the Wild. Since the pucks were put away till next fall, it was a good bet that it was the prospect of profit that was producing the pink.

"Oh, my gosh," Lily gushed. "This would be such a huge contract for me. Not only am I quoting the landscaping design component of

the project, but Eric wants the installation and maintenance quoted, too. Of course, it's all preliminaries, because they have to get the green light on the development first, but Eric said the council was definitely leaning in favor of approval. They're supposed to vote this week."

"Really," I said.

Then how come Alan was giving me the hot potato talk just yesterday and saying that the development was far from being a done deal? Granted, Alan wasn't in the inner circle on this project, but he was a fairly skilled political observer, and I trusted his opinion. Which made me wonder: what did Eric Stodegard know that Alan didn't?

"Actually," she said, pausing dramatically to look at each of us in turn, "Eric said it was in the bag." She paused a minute and then directed a look at Luce that reminded me of some of my female students when they were doing their silent communication thing. Uh oh, I thought. Women bonding. Secret messages. Danger, danger! Stay clear!

"Eric said he and I just might have to spend a lot of time together on this project," she added. "Not that I would mind."

Luce smiled back at Lily. More secret messages. I almost groaned out loud. It was like being in my office at school. I needed to head this off at the pass.

"So why does Stodegard think this project is going to happen?" I asked Lily, deftly steering the conversation away from romantic possibilities and onto firmer, albeit contested, ground. "I heard it wasn't anywhere near being settled. I know there's a citizens' group that's fighting it tooth and nail. They're doing an environmental survey sometime this week to present the results to the council." I took the bottle of steak sauce my mom handed to me and put it on the table next to the salt and pepper shakers.

"Well, all I know is what Eric told me at lunch." Lily turned to Luce. "What did he tell you?"

Wait a minute. Luce had talked with this Stodegard guy about the development? And I didn't know about this, why?

Luce obviously read my mind (which she seems to have the knack of doing, I'd noticed) because she put her arm around my waist and squeezed. "I was going to tell you about it on the way over here, but you were so lost in thought, I let it go," she explained. "Eric dropped in at Maple Leaf last Wednesday to talk with me and Mitch about his development project. Mitch is the general manager at Maple Leaf," she added for my parents' benefit.

"Why would Maple Leaf be involved? Maple Leaf is a conference center," I reminded everyone.

"But our parent company manages resorts, and Eric is the local point man for OEI, the entertainment company who wants the land," Luce said, picking up a pile of paper napkins which she started folding into little swans at each place setting. "OEI wants a five-star hotel on the site, too, so Eric was touring our facilities to take a look at what we've got to offer. Mitch is working up a preliminary proposal to send to OEI. If we get the contract, the Maple Leaf team would be doing the hiring and training at the new hotel."

She put the last napkin swan on the table.

"Nice," Lily told her.

"You should see what she can do with a full-size cloth dinner napkin," I said.

Lily rolled her eyes. "The contract deal, Bobby. Not the swan. It would be a feather in Maple Leaf's cap, not to mention a sweet chunk of change for the parent company."

"I'm the one who gave Lily's name to Eric for landscaping," Luce added.

"OEI?" my dad asked. He flipped the steaks on the grill amid a small blast of smoke and sizzling meat juices. "Who wants it well-done?"

"Outdoor Entertainment Inc.," Lily said. "They're from Chicago. They want to build an amphitheater on the land as the centerpiece of their project, then add on the hotel and some indoor stages for nightclub acts."

A hotel and nightclubs? I hadn't heard that detail. It really shouldn't have surprised me, though. This stretch of the Minnesota River Valley was filled with entertainment venues—the Valleyfair amusement park, Canterbury Park racetrack, Mystic Lake Casino, Elko Speedway, and the annual Renaissance Festival. Now that I thought about it, why wouldn't someone else want a piece of the entertainment pie? And I had to believe that a hotel/amphitheater complex would generate quite a bit of revenue, which would explain the big money that Alan had mentioned. Of course, that money, then, would in turn yield increased tax income for the county, so an approval for the project would ultimately benefit the county's bottom line, big-time. And you know that had to make quite a few government types pretty darn happy.

Unfortunately, though, money wouldn't be the only thing the complex generated. Along with tax funds that might benefit the area, the complex would also generate an enormous amount of traffic, noise and construction, and those were the concerns fueling the opposition of many of the area residents, Alan had told me. Combined with the protests from conservationists and Karl's citizen's group, it was no wonder the development proposal was a hot potato.

In financial terms, there were enormous amounts of money to be gained.

Or lost.

And from a conservation perspective, the stakes were just as high.

Maybe even higher, considering how few pieces of virgin land were receiving protected status these days. In fact, there had just recently been more rumblings at the state Capitol about appropriating a large tract of wetlands along the river valley for new highways and bridges. It was beginning to seem like the MNDot's appetite for new roadways was insatiable, and while I understood the numbers of the growing population and the need for good roads, I drew the line when it came to hacking off pieces of wildlife refuges to meet those needs.

"Isn't that land the old Dandorff farm?" my mom asked, setting down a bowl of her homemade potato salad on the table. "We used to take you kids there to pick pumpkins for Halloween and go for sleigh rides in the winter."

"Yup, that's it," I said. "I've done a lot of birding there, too, over the years. It's near Louisville Swamp. In fact, I thought that a couple of years ago, I heard that Mr. Dandorff was thinking of giving the land to the state for a park."

"There's a good idea," my dad said, bringing the steaks to the table. "I know if I had some land in that river valley, I'd want it preserved for everyone to enjoy. We've lost so much of the native environment over the years that it's a shame not to hang on and preserve what we have left. We owe it to . . ."

"Our children," Lily and I responded in chorus.

Yes, we'd heard that one a few million times growing up. My dad had been an advocate of preserving natural habitat before most people even knew what natural habitat was. In fact, if you looked around town, you could find my dad's name on almost every native land conservation committee, from prairie restoration groups to waterfowl recovery projects. I always figured that was where Lily got her green thumb —from Dad. I, on the other hand, got the Nature Boy genes.

Thinking again about Dandorff's property, I wondered why the plan to donate the land had fallen through. "That would sure make a nice park," I said. "What do you think happened?"

"Money happened," Lily announced. "And lots of it. It's prime real estate, now, Bobby. Dandorff can make a fortune off that land. Three years ago, it was out in the sticks, but the Cities have grown so fast, it's right in the backyard now. All he needs to make a bundle is the council's approval of OEI's project. And, according to Eric, that's going to happen this week."

I waited for Luce to sit down on the old picnic bench, then sat down next to her.

"I don't know that the council will be approving anything this week," I said after a moment. "Nancy Olson was a council member."

"Oh, my," Mom said, sighing. "The poor woman. I wonder what pushed her over the edge."

"Why do you say that?" Lily asked. "She didn't commit suicide, Mom. She was murdered. It's not a question of what, but who."

The rest of us stared at Lily, speechless.

"How do you know that?" I asked. I knew I hadn't called her up and shared Dani's comments with her.

"It was on the radio when I drove over here," she continued. "Nancy Olson was shot in the chest. The police arrested a suspect this morning, but they weren't releasing his name."

"I found a murder victim," my mom breathed.

Gee whiz, could this Mother's Day get any better?

CHAPTER FIVE

My life was over.

It was Monday morning, and there was a policeman waiting outside my office door. My guess was that my work week was going to start with explaining that I hadn't slept with a student.

None of the staff handbooks covered that one.

Then I saw who it was, and I relaxed.

"You just can't stay out of trouble, can you?" Officer Rick Cook greeted me.

"I live for trouble," I said, unlocking my office door and tossing my briefcase on my desk. "Come on in."

Rick is our school police liaison officer—the school cop, in other words. He's also a personal friend of mine and a fellow birder, as well as a Savage High alumnus and former school baseball star. This morning he was in full official cop regalia: uniform pants, shirt, shoes, service revolver, two-way radio clipped on his shoulder, night stick, and TAZER on his belt. The only thing not department issue was the very small diamond stud that Rick wore in his left earlobe.

"Sometimes a fellow just wants to feel pretty," he'd told me when he got back from a Caribbean cruise with his girlfriend, sporting the stud. I suspected there was more to the story, but I had yet to pry it out of him. A wise man knows when to quit asking questions. Especially when the other guy is the one with the gun.

"Scared me for a minute there," I told him. "The full-metal-jack-et look first thing on a Monday is a little tough to take. I assume this is a social call, not business? Because I'm sure you probably already know all about my weekend."

Rick dropped into the chair opposite my desk. "Oh, yeah. You are the talk of the police station, buddy. 'Hey, that counselor at the high school who always gets the speeding violations found another body!' You're famous, Bob. We usually get drunks and the occasional domestic disturbance on weekends, but murder? No way. This is the big time. Much more exciting than writing you tickets."

"I'm glad I made your day, Rick." My reputation with the local police for my history of speeding tickets—always earned while I was birding, I might add—was nothing new, but being known as a body-finder was. "So who got arrested?"

He hesitated for a moment, tapping a finger on the butt of his gun. "Chris Olson."

I sat down hard on my chair and leaned way back to stare at the ceiling. "Dani's brother."

"Yup. But he wasn't arrested. Yet. He was held for questioning and released."

"Do they have evidence?"

"Mostly circumstantial. Opportunity and motive. The trailer Chris lives in is right on Murphy-Hanrehan's border. The stream that passes the trailer eventually empties into the pond where the body was found. The deceased's car was sitting around the corner from the trailer, and Mr. Olson said his wife had told him she was heading out to see Chris on Friday night. And everyone knows there was bad blood between Chris and his mother." He shrugged. "A fight, maybe Chris was drinking, and . . ."

"And?" I leaned forward, my arms on my knees.

"I just don't know, Bob. From what I hear, it looks bad, but Chris a killer?" He shook his head. "I know the family's a mess and Chris's been in trouble before, but I know the kid. Hell, I've brought him in myself for drinking and aggravated assault a couple times. But he's been doing good for the last year, staying out of trouble, keeping his nose clean." Rick's knuckles were practically drumming on his gun butt. "I don't want it to be him. For his sake and Dani's. But so far, he's the man."

I aimed a pointed look at his tapping knuckles, of which he apparently hadn't been aware. As soon as he followed my gaze, he lifted his hand away from his side.

"Sorry," he said. "I'm a little distraught about this."

"Join the club," I told him.

I'd spent a lousy night, tossing and turning, worrying about Dani. Wondering how she was taking her mom's murder. Wondering if she knew more than she was telling. She had, after all, insisted it wasn't Chris. So who did that leave?

Her father.

Granted, Dani hadn't said anything about him, other than that she was afraid to go home when her dad was there, angry. Not exactly a ringing endorsement of paternal security. And though she'd said nothing else, I'd gotten to know her well enough the past few months to know she was holding something back. What that might be, I had no idea.

I suddenly wondered exactly how much the investigators knew about the family. Everything Dani had told me was confidential, so it wasn't my place to offer any information, but man, there was a whole lot of crap going on in that household. The police had to be looking at Mr. Olson, too . . . or at least, they had to be if Dani had given them even some of the details she had shared with me.

Then again, Dani had told them she'd been sleeping with me on Friday night. Her credibility wasn't the best right now, I was sure of that. Which reminded me . . .

"Ah, Rick, by any chance, did my name come up in connection with . . ." I raised my eyebrows in question.

For a second, he flashed a grin. "Yeah, I heard something about that. Don't worry, Bob. Your secret is safe . . . with the entire Savage Police Department."

I groaned. Like that made me feel just a whole lot better. "No one believed Dani, I take it."

"Nah," he replied. "It's pretty common for kids to come up with wild statements the first time they're questioned in cases like this. Max Wilson is the detective in charge, and he knows I work here, so he gave me a buzz on Saturday after he talked with Dani the first time. I vouched for you. Said your girlfriend would kill you if she heard you were fooling around with anyone else, let alone a student. I figure you owe me a beer for going to bat for you."

"Just name the brew. The last thing I need is for that rumor to get started."

"No," he corrected me. "The last thing you need is for that rumor to be true."

I nodded. "Point taken. I knew there was a reason I kept you around, Cook."

Beyond my door, I could hear the other counselors coming in for the day. So far, no students were lined up to see me, so I figured I had a couple more minutes to grill Rick.

"What about Mr. Olson?" I asked, trying to carefully slide around my confidentiality issues. "You and I both know that more often than not, it's the spouse in a case like this."

"Olson has an alibi. He was at the casino. He's a regular, so everyone knows him. Lots of witnesses." Rick touched the stud in his ear. "The department isn't going to let this drag out, I can tell you that. Max wants to make an arrest. If he's going to pick up Chris, I expect it'll happen tomorrow. "

Tomorrow.

I swore silently to myself. Rick said Chris was the man, but he wasn't. Chris was just a kid—maybe nineteen. Had his relationship with his mom hit critical mass and exploded? I guessed that was the police's line of thinking, and from what Rick had said, it sounded like they were getting close to issuing a warrant.

But Dani had insisted Chris was innocent.

"How good is Olson's alibi?" I pressed. "The casino's packed with people, sure, but who's watching a clock? Who knows exactly when anyone comes and goes there?"

Rick tugged on the stud in his ear. "Where are you going with this, Bob?"

"Look, Rick." I leaned forward on my desk. "Chris has been the only one in that family who Dani can count on," I reminded him. "He's practically been her parent for the last year. If he's arrested, what's she going to do?"

I nodded at my office door and Rick reached over to swing it partially shut. It was time to bend a rule a little.

For Dani's sake.

I lowered my voice and looked at Rick. "Did you know that she told me once that when she got home after work one night, her bed was gone? Her dad had hocked it to pay back some gambling debts. She didn't even have a bed to sleep in, Rick. Since Chris moved out, she's been spending a lot of nights at his place. At least there she has a place to sleep and nobody yelling at two in the morning."

Rick leaned forward, too. "I know what you're saying, Bob, but we can't do anything about it. She's only fifteen and without evidence of physical abuse or neglect, we can't do a thing to get her out of her parents' home. Child protection services won't kick in at this point. She'd have to go the legal route and try to get herself emancipated, and I just don't see that happening."

He sighed with the same frustration I felt. "I know Dani. She's a great kid. But we can't help her."

"Yes, we can," I insisted. "If nothing else, we can be here for her. Isn't that why we do what we do? We want to help kids. And Dani's going to need all the help she can get. This much I can do."

I moved my briefcase off my desk and turned on my computer. As soon as it booted up, I was going to schedule an hour every day for Dani to come in. It wasn't much, but at the moment, it was something.

Or at least, it was something until I could figure out a better way to help Dani.

"Mr. White?"

Rick and I turned towards my doorway. Rick reached out and pulled the door completely open. Mandy and Alicia, Dani's best friends, were standing just outside. They both had puffy eyes from crying.

"I'm outta here," Rick said, rising out of the chair. "Catch you later, Bob."

I waved the girls in. Even before they got a word out, they were sniffling.

I pulled out the box of tissues.

Chapter Six

It is so awful! Dani's mom is dead and everyone thinks her brother did it!" Mandy wailed.

"And her dad is such a jerk!" Alicia sobbed.

I pushed the tissue box to the edge of the desk where they could reach it. They both pulled out a handful.

"You know, the best thing you can do for Dani is just be there when she needs to talk. She really needs you two to be strong for her right now," I said.

Yes, it sounded trite, but in this case, it was the best advice I could give them. Apparently, they thought it was good advice, too, because they both sat down, wailed a little more, hugged each other and built little piles of tissues on my floor. That's right—piles of tissues. Like I already said: "Tissues" is my middle name. So right there, you have the short version of the job description for counselors: give trite advice and buy stock in Kleenex.

Although, in my defense, I have to say that the kids don't think my advice is trite. At least, no one has ever said that to me. But then again, that may be because a lot of the time, they aren't even listening to me. Over the years, I've found that few students actually hear what I'm saying because they don't want advice; what they want is to just have someone listen to them. For all they care, I could probably recite the Declaration of Independence as advice, but as long as I listen to what they have to say, they think I'm brilliant.

Okay, that's a humbling thought. As long as I take up space and nod sympathetically, I can wallow in job security. So much for my illusions of counseling grandeur.

"Where is Dani?" I asked, once the deluge had slacked off.

Mandy wiped her nose and pulled her very low-riding jeans almost up to her belly button.

Crap.

She was a dress code violation waiting to happen. Not only was her belly button showing—a definite no-no—but even her hipbones were visible above the top of her jeans. For the millionth time since it had turned May, I silently cursed the clothing manufacturers who designed anything but long sacks for teenage girls. Seriously, between dealing with dress code violations and the onset of spring fever—read "raging hormone season"—among the students, I almost gave up counseling my first year at Savage. I figured zoo-keeping would be less stressful.

"She's at home with her dad," Mandy answered.

"And her dad is such a jerk!" Alicia repeated.

"Do we have to go to class, Mr. White? Can't we just chill here in your office for a while? Please? I am way too upset to go to Biology."

No surprise there. Mandy was always too upset to go to Biology. In fact, the very thought of going to any class upset Mandy. For the life of me, I didn't know how she could get up in the morning just for thinking about going to class.

I blew out a big breath and mentally reviewed my options. I could let them cry in my office for a little. I could send them to class. If I sent Mandy anywhere in those jeans, though, she'd be back in my office in no time. Pay now or pay later?

"Tell you what," I said. "You cover up your stomach with a sweatshirt and I'll give you both ten minutes to chill in here. Then you have to go to class and stay there for the rest of the day. Otherwise, I'll send you to class right now and when you get sent back down here for dress code violation, I'm turning you over to the assistant principal who's going to call your mom. You choose."

Mandy looked at Alicia and, after that same kind of telepathic communication I'd observed between Luce and Lily last night at my parents' place, she pulled a sweatshirt out of her backpack. She knotted it around her middle. Not quite what I had in mind, but it did the trick—the offending body parts were covered.

Meanwhile, Alicia's attention had returned to Dani.

"Poor Dani," she sniffled, starting to cry again. "Her brother was going to fix stuff so she could live with him instead of her parents. Her mom was so mean to her, Mr. White."

"Yeah," Mandy agreed, choking back a sob. "She was always yelling at Dani. And her brother, too. But now what's she going to do? Her brother's going to jail, and her dad is such a jerk."

"Hmm," I said. "I'm getting the distinct impression you girls think Dani's dad is a jerk. Am I getting warm here at all?"

They both looked at me like I was speaking an alien language. I wasn't surprised. Understatement, along with subtlety and (frequently) simple reason, I've found, is typically lost on teenage girls. Especially on teenage girls like Mandy and Alicia who make piles of tissues in my office when they should be in Biology. I gave them their ten minutes, then shuffled them out the door and off to class.

"Yo, Mr. White!"

Karl Solvang headed toward me from across the counseling reception area. With his blond hair and tall athletic frame, he could have been a poster boy for Minnesota All-Americans. His female classmates obviously thought so, too, since he seemed to leave a wake of drooling girls behind him.

I never said spring fever was pretty.

"Mr. White, the potluck was awesome!" Karl announced. "We had thirty people show up, including a couple of the council members. Mr. Dandorff gave us a hayride around his property and told us the history of his farm. Did you know it was one of the first farms in the Minnesota River Valley? There's even the foundation of the original farmhouse still there."

"That's great, Karl. Did you get any commitments from the council members to vote against approval?"

"One for sure. I don't know about the other one. But we're doing the bird survey on Thursday evening. Can you come?"

"Absolutely. We've got a game right after school, but then I'm free for the night."

I'm the assistant coach for the tenth-grade girls' softball team. That means that most days in early May, I'm out on the field after school, coating my cleats with mud and trying not to strangle a bunch of sixteen-year-olds who can't field a ball to save their souls. Not that they don't want to—it's just that their talent is lagging way behind their competitive drive. More than once, I've found that an evening of relaxed birding does wonders for my disposition after an afternoon with the softball team.

"That's great, Mr. White," Karl was saying. "Do any of your birding friends want to come, too? We could use all the people we can find. Mr. Dandorff's property is plenty big."

"I'll see who I can round up," I promised him.

"Hi, Karl."

A girl, obviously part of Karl's fan club, sidled up next to him and gave him a huge smile. "How did the potluck go?"

"It was great!" he told her. "You should have been there."

"I wish I had."

"Yeah, me too."

And then they just stood there looking at each other.

For crying out loud. So much for hanging a "Spring Fever Safe Zone" banner across my door.

I cleared my throat, and I guess Karl's blood started to flow to his brain again.

"Hey," he said, turning his smile back to me, "Gotta run, Mr. White. Later!"

Karl and the girl left, Karl talking and the girl still smiling. Her name was Bridget, I remembered. She was one of my outfield misfits,

but she was showing some real promise at bat, which would be really good for the team, since she was the only left-handed player we had. Some extra evenings in the batting cage, along with a little technique work, and I figured she'd have a swing to reckon with. Maybe we'd even get on the board this year.

Like I already said, birders are nothing if not optimists.

I turned back into my office and closed the door for a little quiet time and space.

I put my tissue box away on the shelf and wondered when Dani would be back in school. I also wondered how Chris was managing, waiting for the police to show up at his door with a warrant for his arrest. Rick hadn't said anything about a murder weapon being found, or if he knew if Chris had an alibi. But Nancy Olson's car sitting around the corner from Chris's trailer certainly didn't bode well for a defense. Did Chris have a gun? I sure hoped not, but the fact was that a lot of my students and their families were hunters; every winter when deer season opened, we had to remind students not to bring rifles onto school property in their cars.

Of all the things Rick had said, though, the one that nagged at the corners of my mind the most was that Chris's own dad told the police that his wife was heading for their son's place that night. Hadn't he realized the implications of what he was saying, that he was laying an incriminating piece of evidence at the feet of the police? Did the man have no instinct to protect his child?

Well, duh, I told myself. How many times had Dani told me about her mother hurling insults at her, reducing her to tears, while her dad ignored the whole scene? I knew the man was ineffective, but was he totally oblivious, too? Why didn't he stand up for Chris? The kid was being suspected of murder!

Unless—and this thought hit me like a ton of bricks—Olson had a reason for shuffling the police straight to Chris. And I could think of only one reason why he'd want that: to take the heat off himself.

Which made me wonder again about that alibi Rick had mentioned.

How good could it be? From what I'd seen the one time I'd been in a casino, nobody was watching a clock. And there weren't any clocks on the walls, either. Losing track of time when you were concentrating on cards had to be even easier than losing money. So who could say for certain when Olson had played at the tables? My understanding of gambling addictions was that, like any addiction, they tended to narrow the addicts' awareness of other circumstances. Things like time and priorities got sucked into the addiction, altering behavior as well as memories.

Dani had told me about the fights between her parents about her dad's gambling—those at two in the morning, as well as the evening shouting matches that preceded her dad's nightly departure for the casino. I knew that money was tight, that Olson had gambled away funds the family couldn't afford to lose. I knew about Dani's bed going for cash to pay gambling debts. And I also knew that addiction was an illness.

What I didn't know, though, was the extent to which Olson's illness might drive him. Dani had said her parents shouted, but she had never mentioned physical abuse between them. Could Olson have finally snapped in the heat of verbal battle and pulled out a gun? Chased his wife down and shot her? That seemed like an extraordinary leap in magnitude of violence, though. Generally, family violence escalated gradually, in stages.

Then again, maybe Dani hadn't told me everything there was to tell about her parents' battles. Experienced counselors know that kids will go to extreme lengths to protect their parents, even those parents whose actions, or lack thereof, are tearing a family apart. No kid wants to unveil the violence in her own home. If Dani's parents had come to bodily blows in the past, then a fatal assault was more . . . not understandable, but not as surprising.

Yet Nancy Olson wasn't beaten to death, I reminded myself. She hadn't been choked. The cause of death was a bullet in her chest. In a case of family violence, that seemed to speak of deliberation, or preparation. Or even, perhaps, just simple anticipation. Self-protection, maybe? How abusive was Nancy Olson? I'd never met either of Dani's parents, so I had no idea what kind of spousal relationship existed, except for the bits Dani had told me. If her dad had shot her mother, was it a crime of passion, self-preservation, or an act of premeditation?

For that matter, the same questions could be asked of Chris. He'd been thrown out of the house by his mom. Had he been looking for retribution? What had Alicia said? Something about Chris fixing things so Dani could live with him instead of their parents. Dani had mentioned something similar herself in the last few weeks. But what could a nineteen-year-old do to accomplish that? Rick said that Chris had cleaned up his act in the last year. That certainly couldn't hurt. But what kind of legal recourse could he have to assist his sister? Was there some way he could have her removed from their parents? Was he working with someone in the county social services?

Or did he have in mind another way to "fix things"?

As I recalled, Chris Olson hadn't been the model of patient forbearance when he'd been at Savage. Nor was he a stranger to alcohol and assault, as Rick had pointed out. Not a good combination even when you weren't topping a detective's list of murder suspects. Of course Dani would defend him.

He was all she had.

Before I could even begin to pursue that train of thought, there was one sharp knock on my door before it swung open.

"Mr. White."

It was my boss, the assistant principal Mr. Lenzen. Mister Stickler-for-policies-rules-and-discipline. That's putting it nicely. If I didn't put it nicely, I'd say he was an ass. He saw everything in black and white—no grays allowed. He had no interest in mitigating circumstances, no tolerance for creative problem-solving, and absolutely no sense of humor.

And I have a feeling he didn't like me very much, either.

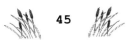

"Mr. Lenzen," I replied, putting on my be-nice-to-your-boss counselor's face. "What can I do for you?"

Mr. Lenzen pulled his starched white handkerchief out of his suit pants pocket and lightly dusted the seat of the chair before he sat down.

Make that anal, as well as an ass.

He carefully folded the handkerchief in his hand. "Is it true that you discovered Mrs. Olson in the marsh?"

"No."

He gave me a sharp look of disbelief.

"My mom did."

Mr. Lenzen narrowed his eyes.

I sighed in surrender. He'd obviously heard the stories already circulating in the staff lounge. "I happened to be with her at the time."

It didn't take a rocket scientist to know where this was going. Mr. Lenzen hated to see the name of Savage High School even remotely associated with anything that might possibly be construed as negative—he took it as a personal affront, as well as the kiss of death for any upcoming school bond issue. He'd probably broken out in a cold sweat and experienced shortness of breath when he heard I was connected to the discovery of Mrs. Olson's body. If it had been up to him, I would have lost my job two months ago because of my involvement in the murder investigation up in Duluth. The thought that I was now associated with another murder case was probably keeping his blood pressure sky-high.

Did I care?

Not really.

On the other hand, I felt like I did owe him a little payback for all the grief he'd put me through when that case had been going down.

"Yes, that's right," I said, feeling my inner evil twin grinning from ear to ear at Mr. Lenzen's discomfort. "I was there. Having been through this kind of thing before, though,"—I couldn't resist jerking his chain a little tighter—"and that being so recently, too, I knew what to expect, and being the model citizen I am, I was more than happy to oblige the police by giving them all the information I could."

I smiled broadly at him. "I made sure they spelled your name right, Mr. Lenzen."

His face actually went pale. I had to bite the inside of my cheek to keep from laughing out loud.

"You're treading on very thin ice, Mr. White," he said. "One involvement in a murder investigation by a member of my staff was one more than I ever cared to hear about. The fact that you were instrumental in solving that case and apprehending a killer is the redeeming reason you're still in this office. Don't push your luck. I highly recommend you stay out of this and just focus on doing your job here."

Gee, I thought the reason I was still in my office was because I was so incredibly good at what I did: taking up space, listening, and handing out tissues. That, and the fact that Mr. Lenzen had managed to squeeze in his own ten seconds of local sound-byte fame commenting on my involvement in the Duluth case. Don't bite the hand that feeds you good press, Mr. Lenzen, I wanted to say, but of course, I didn't.

"I'll keep it in mind," I said instead.

"Good," he said, rising out of the chair. "And, by the way, I believe one of your students, Mandy Walters, is in violation of dress code today. I could see her navel."

"Already taken care of," I assured him.

Just in case, though, I gave a quick try at sending Mandy a telepathic communication of my own to keep that sweatshirt securely wrapped around her middle.

Or failing that, to at least stay out of Mr. Lenzen's sight.

"You'll be happy to know that Savage High is safe from navel exposure for another day, Mr. Lenzen."

He gave me a parting glance of disdain and left.

I waited till he was well out of earshot.

"And if Dani needs me, I'm going to be there for her, Mr. Lenzen. Whether you like it or not."

Man, do I love Mondays.

CHAPTER SEVEN

"Don't pull away from the ball," I said over and over. "Be tough. Assert your authority. Step up to the plate and nail that sucker."

Team practice was over, and I was staying late to coach Bridget and another girl in the batting cage. Together, they'd taken about a hundred swings, and while neither had found their bats' sweet spots, I could see some real improvement in their form. The sucker had yet to be nailed, but I was pretty sure its days were numbered. Combined with the good work I'd seen in the outfield during drills this afternoon, I was even beginning to think there just might be hope for my Savage Bass this season.

Yes, Savage Bass it is. This is Minnesota, after all, land of 10,000 lakes and at least twice that many fishermen, so bass as the school mascot makes perfect sense. I guess somebody along the way decided that Savage Big-mouth Bass was too long a moniker, so we just go with Savage Bass. It makes for great cheers, too. There's the one that goes, "We're the Savage Bass, gonna gobble you up. Gulp! Gulp! Gulp! Gulp!"

Okay, maybe you have to be there to appreciate that one.

My personal favorite is, "We're the big bad Bass, gonna bite your ass!" Of course, the students can't say "ass" because it's a high school game, and the state athletics league frowns on obscenity in cheers, but everyone hears it in their heads anyway. When the kids yell it, they say "ssshh" in place of "ass," so you get, "We're the big bad Bass,

48

gonna bite your ssshh." I've even seen Mr. Lenzen yelling the cheer a few times, heavy on the "ssshh." The man may be anal, but at least he's got a pair of lungs on him.

"Okay, ladies," I told Bridget and Sara after the last ball from the pitching machine crossed the plate untouched. "Let's call it a night."

The girls packed up their bags while I collected the bats to return to the storage locker in the gym. When I stepped back outside the cage, Bridget was waiting for me.

"So Karl says you're coming out to my grandpa's for the bird survey."

I started walking towards the gym. "Your grandpa?"

"Yup. Fritz Dandorff is my grandpa. It's his farm that everybody wants."

"So I've heard."

"It's really getting complicated, though, Coach. Since my grandma died, I think it's hard for my grandpa to make decisions." Bridget pulled her athletic bag higher on her shoulder.

"What do you mean?"

"Well, it's like he used to make up his mind and that was that. Now he's got all these people pressuring him to do what they want, and he says that he isn't sure what's the right thing to do without grandma, because she was his North Star—that all he had to do was look at her and he knew where he was going."

I stopped on the path and studied my—hopefully—future home run hitter. "Sounds like your grandma and grandpa really had something special together, Bridget. It's got to be hard now on your grandpa not to have your grandma around."

She tugged her batting glove off and tucked it into a side pocket of her bag.

"Yeah, it is. And these people aren't helping when they keep bugging him about the land. This realtor guy came over last week one night after dinner when I was at Grandpa's for some batting practice."

49

She smiled up at me. "Could you tell I'd been getting some extra help with my stance? Grandpa and his friend Mr. Ray have been giving me some pointers. They played in a city ball league a long time ago, when they were a lot younger."

"I thought there was something different there," I said. "You're digging your heel in more."

"Grandpa showed me that," she said. "Anyway, this guy showed up and started saying how pleased some E-I-E-I-O company was that he was going to sell the farm and that Grandpa could start making his vacation plans to Tahiti because he was going to be able to afford to go anywhere he wanted."

"Does your grandpa want to go to Tahiti?"

Bridget shook her head. "No. That's just it—I don't think he really wants to go anywhere. Not without Grandma. But I don't think he wants to stay there any more either. Because Grandma's not there. You know?"

I didn't. I hadn't been married for a good fifty years like the Dandorffs had been. It did make me wonder, however, what it would be like to wake up next to Luce for fifty years. Pretty nice, I figured. We could eat scones and go birding.

I started walking again.

Damn. Now that I thought about it, fifty years of Luce and scones and birding sounded really good to me.

Better than good.

I stopped walking again.

And it hit me like a wild pitch.

I wanted to marry Luce.

"Look!"

Bridget pointed past my shoulder to a flock of big white birds spiraling high over the Savage athletic fields. They seemed to float up with the air currents, wafting slowly northward.

"American White Pelicans," I told her, smiling. "They're migrating. When they fly together like that, you call them a kettle."

JAN DUNLAP

"They look kind of confused to me," Bridget observed. "Like they're going in circles. Are you sure they know which way they're going?"

"They know," I assured her. We walked the last few yards to the gym's back door. "It might look like they're all over the place, but they've got their own North Star inside them to tell them where they need to go. Don't worry, Bridget, your grandpa will figure things out."

Just like I had. Finally.

I was going to marry Luce.

Bridget dumped her bag against the side of the building. "I know he will. Eventually. But this realtor guy seems really pushy, and then when Dani's mom showed up, too, she and this guy kind of got into it in front of my grandpa and Mr. Ray and me."

"What?" I dragged my attention back to what Bridget was saying. "Dani's mom was there?"

"My grandpa knew she was coming over. I guess he'd talked to her earlier. She really wants . . ." Bridget glanced at the ground for a second, apparently remembering that Nancy Olson wasn't wanting anything anymore.

"I mean," she continued, " she *wanted* him to tell these E-I-E-I-O guys to get lost. She thinks—thought—the county needs more parks or something."

"It's OEI, Bridget. Not E-I-E-I-O."

"Whatever. Anyway, this realtor guy got really mean and told Dani's mom to get out of the way, that the property deal meant too much revenue to the county for her to try to stop it from happening. And then Grandpa told them both to leave."

Jeez Louise. My future home-run hitter had morphed into an investigator's goldmine of information. Did Detective Wilson know any of this stuff? If he didn't, he needed to. And if he did, he'd have to hold off on arresting Dani's brother Chris.

Wouldn't he?

I put my hand on Bridget's shoulder. "Have you told anyone about Mrs. Olson and the realtor coming to see your grandpa last week?"

She squinted up at me. "No. Why?"

I shrugged my shoulders. "No reason. Just curious."

And just thinking I was going to call Rick as soon as I had a moment alone so I could tell him everything she'd just told me. He could pass it along to Detective Wilson, who I expected would then want to take a quick trip out to the farm to talk with Bridget's grandpa himself. If there had been some verbal fireworks going off between Nancy Olson and the realtor—who, I assumed, was none other than Lily's Eric Stodegard—then maybe Wilson could find a good reason or two to wait before he named Chris the designated killer. Given what Bridget had said, maybe the detective would even find a whole new ballpark to play in.

Because judging from Bridget's comments, I had a feeling that batting practice wasn't the only game going on down at the farm.

E-I-E-I-O.

CHAPTER EIGHT

Hey, Coach."

I slammed shut the door to my SUV's back seat where I'd just dumped my gym bag and turned around to find Dave Janssen smiling at me from behind the wheel of his Ford pickup.

"Hi, Dave. What's up?"

"Not a lot. I'm just on my way to a meeting and thought I'd swing by to see if our Lady Bass are ready for the game with Drake on Wednesday night. Big rivalry, you know. I'm hoping to clear my schedule so I can be in the stands to cheer our girls on."

Dave's an insurance agent and the father of two boys at Savage. He's also been one of the most active members of the sports booster club over the years. Whether his boys are playing or not, Dave is the Bass fan you can't miss at any game, because he always wears his Go Bass hat.

Nothing special, really. Just a fishing hat.

With a foot-long rubber bass attached.

That lights up when Savage scores.

Go Bass.

I leaned against my car. "We're ready, Dave. The girls are psyched."

Which was a very good thing, considering that they didn't have much of anything else to work with. Enthusiasm, yes.

Natural ability, not so much.

"Glad to hear it," he replied. "You know, when we get that new entertainment complex in here, we're going to see some increasing school funds, mark my words. I know a lot of folks are worried about the impact on the quality of life around here, but we can stand to give up a little open space that isn't doing anybody any good right now, anyway." He waved a hand out his window towards the ball fields behind me. "I know for a fact that there are a lot of people in this community—Bass Boosters, every one of them—who would be happy to see some major improvements to our athletic facilities here at the high school. I know I would. Wouldn't you, Coach?"

"It'd be nice," I hedged, suddenly remembering that Janssen had been elected to the county council last fall, which meant he had to be in the thick of the Dandorff land deal. "But I'm not sure that's the price I want to pay—tearing up some beautiful natural habitat just so we can upgrade our sports facilities. Sounds like a losing proposition in the long term, if you ask me."

"Well, you might be right."

Janssen was doing some hedging of his own, I noted. Then again, he was not only a salesman, but a politician as well. I wondered where he really stood on the land deal, or if he even had a position on it at all.

"I hear the council is voting on the entertainment complex this week," I said. "Can you do that, missing a member now? Or do you just appoint someone to fill in Nancy Olson's vacancy?"

Janssen absently patted the casing on his side-view mirror. A glint of sun reflected from the gun rack behind his head. "You know, I'm not sure. Never had to worry about that before." He shook his head. "I knew Nancy had problems at home, but I never imagined . . . you just never know, do you?"

"I guess not."

He checked his rearview mirror and started rolling forward. He stuck a hand out the window to wave. "See you Wednesday, Coach."

I watched him drive out the school parking lot and turn towards town. Man, I was beginning to feel like everyone had a stake in the

Dandorff property deal. The city wanted the revenue. Conservationists wanted the property. My sister stood to get a big chunk of business. Dave Janssen and the other parents in the booster club wanted new athletic fields. I wanted a protected place to bird for years to come.

Good things, all of them, even if they did generate conflict within a community. I climbed into the car and put the gear in reverse. Heck, I could think of lots of cities in America that would probably give anything to have Savage's problems. We didn't have gang wars, rampant unemployment, unchecked vandalism or drive-by shootings.

We did have dress code violations, and we did have a murder of a councilwoman, but the more I heard from others about Nancy Olson and her dysfunctional family, the more I thought it likely that her death was the result of a family breaking point, and not part of a political conspiracy.

Political conspiracy?

In Savage?

Home of the Lady Bass and Dave Janssen's Go Bass hat?

What was I thinking?

Wham!

I looked in my rearview mirror to see that I had backed into one of the trash bins against the gym wall.

Obviously, I wasn't thinking at all.

CHAPTER NINE

It was after seven o'clock by the time I finally made it into my kitchen to put together some dinner. I heated up the leftover lasagna that Luce had brought over last week and checked the MOU messages in my email. Someone had seen a Golden-crowned Kinglet and a Veery, neither of which were on my most-wanted list, so I deleted those messages and tried to scan through the other twenty sightings that had been posted in the course of the day. Three warbler sightings were noteworthy: a Northern Parula, a Pine Warbler, and a Louisiana Waterthrush. I figured I could chase the Parula on Tuesday evening if I left softball practice right when it was over and didn't stay to work with Bridget. If I found the Parula quickly, I might be able to try for the Pine then, too. The Waterthrush was out at Louisville Swamp, and since I would be out there Thursday evening doing the survey with Karl's group, that would be the time to chase it. I finished dinner, cleaned up, talked briefly on the phone with Luce and went to bed.

I didn't ask her to marry me.

Yet.

I needed some time to come up with a better proposal than comparing us to ducks.

Maybe I should ask Alan for some ideas.

Then again, maybe not.

I was just on my way out to the deck to refill the bird feeders when the doorbell rang. Cutting back through the house, I caught a

glimpse through the foyer windows of someone sitting on my front step. I opened the door.

"Hi, Mr. White."

"Dani."

"Is Mr. Thunderhawk here?"

"No. Just me."

"Oh," she said. "I didn't want to . . . you know . . . be interfering."

"Dani," I said. "Mr. Thunderhawk is my best friend. We've known each other for a very long time. That's all."

"Oh," she said again. "Okay. Can we talk?"

"Sure." I sat down beside her on the step. There was no way I was asking her into the house. If Dani was going to show up at my door, I wanted the whole neighborhood to hear our conversation. Better yet, I wanted it taped and televised to a national audience. I figured it was the only way I could be guaranteed that license plates stayed out of my foreseeable future.

Dani pulled her knees up to her chest and locked her arms around them.

"I never wanted my mother to die."

"Of course, you didn't," I assured her. "No one has said that about you, Dani."

"But it's really weird, now, Mr. White. I can sleep at home and it's quiet all night long." She paused. "My mom and dad aren't yelling at each other anymore. I don't feel like I'm waiting all the time for my mom to start ragging at me. And my dad is different, too." She looked up at me. "He bought me a new bed—a really fancy one. It's got a headboard and shelves and everything. He said he's on a winning streak at the casino."

Nancy Olson wasn't even buried yet, and her husband was back at the gaming tables. I shook my head in pure disgust, but didn't say anything. Right now, Dani didn't need me to criticize her father; she needed someone to just be with her. She sat silently for a few moments, her fingers plucking at the hem of her jeans.

"My brother didn't shoot my mother," she finally said. "I know that's what everyone's saying, but he didn't do it."

"Have you told the police that?" I asked. "Did you tell them everything about your family, Dani?"

I could see the tears starting in her eyes.

"No," she whispered. "They don't ask me about my mom. They don't ask me about Chris. They just keep asking me when my dad left for the casino the night before and when he got home. That first time when they came to the house, after she was dead, I told them I was here with you, so I didn't know anything about my dad. Then when the police came back yesterday, I told them I didn't see my dad until he got up about eleven o'clock in the morning."

"Did you tell the police where you were Friday night?"

She sniffed and nodded, her eyes still on her jeans. "I'm so afraid, Mr. White. My dad would get really angry with my mom, but he never hit her or anything. I can't think he might have hurt her. But if Chris didn't kill her, then who else was there?"

She brushed some tears from the corners of her eyes. "He's my dad, Mr. White. He couldn't kill my mom." She looked up at me, silently begging me to agree with her. "Could he?"

This was something I obviously had missed in Crisis Counseling 610. I had no idea what to say. Grief support I could manage, but dealing with a family death that was ruled a murder and possibly the result of in-home violence was clearly out of my league. Nor could I share with Dani what I'd learned from Bridget about her mother's run-in with Stodegard and my growing suspicion that more was involved in Nancy's death than family meltdown. Besides, throwing blame on other people wouldn't make Nancy Olson any less dead or her daughter's pain any less real. So I did what every wise counselor, when faced with an impasse, did.

I passed the buck.

"Dani," I said gently, "I think it would be really helpful for you to talk with Ms. Theis again. As the school psychologist, she has a lot more experience with grieving than I do."

"No," she said, shaking her head. "No."

"Look, Dani—" I started to explain, but she cut me off.

"No, you look." She pulled herself up straight on the step and leveled a glare right in my face. "I need you, Mr. White. I need you to help my brother. He didn't kill my mom. If everyone knew that, then I could live with him, instead of with my dad. You've got to help him so I can live with him, Mr. White. You're the only person I know who can help us."

Talk about timing. Finally, after all these weeks of my counseling Dani to be more assertive and let people know what she wanted and needed, she was doing it.

Unfortunately, she was doing it with me.

Even so, part of me wanted to sing the "Hallelujah Chorus." It's not often I get to see my counseling efforts result in real behavioral change so quickly. Hearing Dani speak up for herself was like hearing the full-throated song of the first warbler of spring after a long cold winter.

The other part of me, however, was wishing for a mute button. That part of me was remembering Mr. Lenzen's newest warning. Suddenly, I felt very attached to my little closet of an office.

"Dani, I'm not a police officer, and I'm not a detective," I gently reminded her. "You have to tell the police what you know and let them do their job. They'll clear your brother."

If they can, I added silently to myself.

I thought briefly about my call to Rick after I'd locked up the gym. He'd promised to contact Wilson and pass along Bridget's story about Stodegard and Nancy Olson. Rick had guessed that the detective would be on his way to talk with Mr. Dandorff within the hour. I hoped he was right. I also hoped that Wilson found all kinds of reasons to keep investigating Nancy Olson's murder and just as many reasons not to arrest her son.

But Dani wasn't buying.

"No," she repeated. "I need you. You have to help me. You're always saying you're there for me, so be there, Mr. White. Help me."

She was right. I was always saying that.

My mistake.

Because now I had the—opportunity?—to put my money where my mouth was.

Opportunity.

Not responsibility. What Dani was asking of me clearly went beyond my professional obligations.

What Dani was asking of me, however, was not beyond my personal sense of responsibility.

If Dani needed me, I was going to be there.

And if push came to shove, and Mr. Lenzen kicked me out of Savage, certainly there were other closet-sized offices that might welcome me somewhere.

But more than any concerns about job security, I suddenly found myself thinking about my own growing-up years. Thanks to my parents, I'd never had to experience a moment of doubt about who I could trust and who would come through for me when I needed someone. My mom and dad were the bedrock of my world. Dani, on the other hand, seemed to have grown up surrounded by quicksand. The two people who should have been the most solid and supportive in her life had failed her miserably.

And I'd be damned before I joined that little club.

"Okay, Dani," I finally said. "Here's the deal: you see Ms. Theis tomorrow, and I'll go talk with your brother to see what I can do. It may turn out to be not much, but I'm willing to try."

Dani let out a big sigh and tried to smile but couldn't quite manage it. She looked spent, and I was sure her standing up to me had used up a whole supply of adrenaline and nerve she hadn't even realized she had. I hoped she slept well tonight in that fancy new bed of hers.

Man, was I proud of her.

"Okay, Mr. White," she said. "Deal. Thanks. Really. Thanks."

"Don't thank me yet," I told her. "I haven't done anything."

Overhead, the honking of a flock of Canada Geese floated through the evening air, and I asked Dani if she needed a ride home. Thankfully, she didn't, because otherwise I was going to have to call Alan or Rick to do a ride-along since I still had this residual fear of orange jumpsuits.

Dani pulled out her cell phone and made a call. I didn't mean to listen in, but since she was sitting next to me, I couldn't help but hear her half of the conversation.

"Mandy's picking you up?" I choked out.

I wondered if she could hear the note of raw fear in my voice. I know I heard it. The idea of Mandy behind any wheel was frightening enough, but the thought that she was loose on the roads in my neighborhood was more than enough to keep me out of the car. The girl didn't know the meaning of "attention span." Unless her powers of concentration in a car were astronomically better than those she displayed—or rather, didn't display—in her Biology class, the entire city of Savage might as well consider itself under siege and just stay home.

I wondered how long I could hold out. Did I have enough bread?

Birdseed?

Beer?

Suddenly I was glad I had all those store magnets on my fridge. I'd have to check and see who delivered.

"She turned sixteen last week," Dani said. "And she has this really great car her parents gave her. She said I could borrow it when I get my license next month. She's such a great friend, Mr. White. Only a really good friend would let you borrow her car."

Only a really good friend whose parents didn't know what their daughter was doing with it, I silently added.

"So," Dani said, sliding a shy look up at me. "You and Mr. Thunderhawk aren't gay?"

CHAPTER TEN

I opened my eyes and stared at the ceiling of my bedroom.

It was morning.

Or at least, it'd be at some point. Right now, however, wasn't it.

I reached over to the phone that was ringing on my nightstand. "Hello?"

"Bob! You gotta listen to this!"

It was Tom Hightower, one of my best birding buddies from Bloomington. I glanced at my bedside alarm clock.

It was 5:22 a.m.

A bird's song came clearly over the phone: loud, clear and with a distinctive slurring at the end.

It was a Hooded Warbler.

"Did you hear it?" Tom was back on the line, excitement flooding his voice. "I was on my way home from work and had a hunch to check out this old picnic area near the woods by Hyland to see if any warblers were singing, and jeez! A Hooded Warbler!"

"It's early," I said, rubbing my hand over my eyes. Even as I said it, though, the darkness in my room was beginning to lighten. It must have been close to sunrise. Shoot. There was no way I was going to get back to sleep before I had to get up for work.

"Yes! I know!" Tom's voice rang out over the phone. "I usually don't see a Hooded Warbler till late May at the earliest. This is really early for me!"

"I meant the time, Tom. Not the bird."

"Oh. Right." He paused a moment. "What time is it anyway?"

I watched the numbers shimmer and change on my clock. "It's five-thirty," I told him.

"Hah! Guess it's true—the early bird gets the worm. Or in this case, the early birder gets the Hooded Warbler. Post it for me?"

"Sure." I rolled to a sitting position on the edge of my bed. Since I wasn't going to get any more sleep, I figured I might as well post Tom's sighting on the MOU net for any other early birders who might be on their way out. It's always gratifying to tell other birders when a hunch leads to a good bird.

Hopefully, Tom wasn't the only one with good hunches this morning. Detective Wilson came to mind.

Rick had called me back late last night, saying that Wilson had seemed pretty stoked about the information I had passed along. With any luck, the good detective was busy formulating some new plans for his own hunt this morning, none of which led to arresting Chris Olson for his mother's murder. Otherwise, thanks to my promise to Dani, I was going to have a lot of territory to cover today—if Chris was in jail, I was going to have to find Dani and take her with me in hopes I could speak with him. If I had to take Dani with me, I'd have to find someone else to ride along with us as a chaperone. If I had to find someone else to go with us as chaperone, I'd probably have to go pick that person up first.

It was only five-thirty in the morning, and I was tired already.

I needed a double espresso.

Within the hour, I pulled my SUV into a parking spot at the Joy of Java and headed into the shop. As usual, it was packed with loyal customers getting their caffeine fix on their way into work. I ordered my espresso, moved past the bakery case to pick up my order, and almost collided with another customer who'd just gotten her coffee.

It was my sister Lily. "What are you doing here?"

She looked up at me from under the sweep of her auburn hair. "Drinking coffee. What does it look like I'm doing?"

I snagged my own drink from the counter and followed her through the morning crowd. "I mean, why here? Don't you usually go to that coffee shop around the corner from Lily's Landscaping?"

"Yeah, I do. But I'm meeting someone here this morning," she said over her shoulder.

"Pretty early. Business or pleasure?"

She stopped at an empty table against the back wall of the shop and put her drink down. "Go away, Bobby. This is a table for two and you're not invited."

I pulled out the chair and sat down.

"I am now."

Lily sat down across from me and took a sip of her coffee. "I'm meeting Eric. He wants to see the numbers I ran for the landscaping proposal before he takes them to OEI."

I circled my cup with both hands and enjoyed the feeling of the heat seeping into my palms. It reminded me of Alan's description of the council's attitude towards the entertainment complex.

"It's a hot potato," I told Lily. "This whole deal. Alan told me there's a lot of conflicting opinions on whether or not it should go forward." I gave her a warning look. "Don't count your chickens before they hatch, Lily."

"I'm not counting anything." She leaned towards me over the little tabletop. "But I'm also not going to let a great contract pass me by because I didn't pursue it. It's business, Bobby. Eric says it's going to happen. Someone's going to get the landscaping contract, so why shouldn't it be me?"

Her attention shifted to the counter across the room.

"Here comes Eric now. Be nice." She smiled and waved at the dark-haired man in the expensive-looking suit who was weaving his way to our table.

"How nice?"

She kicked my shin under the table.

"You can leave now."

I stood up and waited for the realtor to reach us.

"Morning, Lily," he said, his smile bright and broad. Then he turned to me, holding his hand out to shake mine. "Eric Stodegard. I don't believe we've met, though you look familiar to me."

I watched his eyes dart from my face to Lily's and then back again. Recognition dawned. "Ah. You must be the little brother. It's Bob, right?"

Little?

Unless the espresso had suddenly not only stunted my growth but actually reversed it, I was pretty sure I had at least six inches on the guy.

Before I could open my mouth, though, Lily took control of the conversation.

"So, Bobby, we don't want to keep you from getting to school. I know you have tons to do with seniors graduating. Getting them off to college. Into technical schools. Training programs. Fast food career tracks."

"You work at Savage High School?" Eric asked, apparently oblivious to what Lily was trying to do, which was get rid of me.

"I'm a counselor there."

Eric nodded. "You know that Olson kid? The one who killed his mother?"

I frowned at the cup of coffee in my hand. Gee, was this guy just naturally a jerk or did he have to work at it?

"I don't know Chris Olson personally," I said. "But no one's accused him of murder."

Yet.

That I knew of.

"If you ask me, that kid was just a disaster waiting to happen. Everyone on the council knew about the problems Nancy was having with him. He was making her life hell. They might as well lock that kid up and throw away the key. Hopeless is my guess."

He placed his coffee on the table and smiled warmly at Lily.

She smiled back.

I could have sworn the room was getting warmer.

For crying out loud. It was bad enough I had to deal with teens with spring fever, but my own sister?

For a second, I tried to see Stodegard through Lily's eyes. Sure, the guy was good-looking, successful, sophisticated. No wedding band. Why shouldn't she be attracted to him? I was the one with the OEI problem, not Lily. And the guy really did have perfect teeth. His parents must have spent a boatload on braces, I thought.

The orthodontist's boat, I mean.

"What have you got for me, Lily?" His voice dropped to an almost intimate note. "Let's take it nice and slow, because I don't want to miss a thing."

Oh—and about those braces?

I hoped they had hurt like hell.

For years.

And that he still had to wear a retainer at night.

I didn't care what Lily saw. The man was a jerk. He'd made himself judge and jury for a boy he didn't even know, and now he was hitting on my sister, blatantly.

Tom Hightower was wrong, I decided, turning to leave. The early bird doesn't always catch the worm.

Sometimes it catches a snake.

CHAPTER ELEVEN

As soon as I got into my office, I quit thinking of ways to torpedo Lily's budding romance and started focusing on what I could do to help Chris Olson. I shot off an email to Alan to ask him what he knew of Dani's brother. If I was going to have to go to bat for the boy today, I wanted to be as well prepared as possible with whatever information I could find about him. Surprises would not be good. The fact that Stodegard claimed that everyone on the council was aware of the bad blood between Nancy and her son wasn't making me feel very confident about painting Chris as a model citizen; knowing that Janssen had made a similar comment last evening only reinforced that feeling.

On the other hand, I hadn't heard from either Dani or Rick this morning, so I was hoping that meant that Chris was still a free man. At this point, any delay in his arrest had to be good news. While a little birdie hadn't whispered in my ear that Wilson had dropped Chris as his prime suspect, I was willing to bet that after speaking with Dandorff last night, the detective was taking a closer look at the players in the property deal.

At least, that's what I was counting on.

Yeah, I know. I'd just told Lily this morning not to count her chickens before they hatched, and here I was doing the same thing. Just because I give good advice doesn't mean I always take it.

It's sort of like that "Physician, heal thyself" thing—"Counselor, counsel thyself."

Or is it the blind leading the blind?

You can lead a horse to water, but you can't make him drink?

I shook my head. It was going to be another long day.

By the time the second class period rolled around, I'd finished off two more cups of coffee when Alan walked into my office.

"Don't you have a class to teach?" I asked.

"Nope." Alan dropped into the chair. "It's my prep hour. Under the present circumstances, I thought our little chat about Chris was better held in private." He reached back and swung my door shut.

"What do you know about Chris?"

"Chris Olson used to be a loose cannon. He had anger management issues, problems with authority figures and a drinking problem. And that was on a good day."

I sat back and whistled.

"But," Alan continued, "you'll note I said 'used to be.' He and I finally had it out in class one day the spring of his sophomore year— maybe four years ago now. He'd lipped off once too many times to me, and I called him on it. I grabbed him by the collar and pulled him out in the hall and asked him what the hell he was doing with his life."

Both of my eyebrows shot up. "You have got to be kidding, Alan. Teachers get fired for that."

"At the time, I didn't care. I'd had it with him. Especially since he was plenty bright and I hate to see kids waste what they can do."

Alan's dark-brown eyes drifted away from my face to focus on a point somewhere behind me—somewhere in the past, I thought. When we'd roomed together in college, there'd been more than one night when he'd talked late into the darkness about growing up on the reservation. Some of the memories were good, some not. But either way, they'd made him decide to push himself through high school, and then college, and then grad school, while so many of his childhood acquaintances dropped out and never became the men and women he imagined they could be.

"I told him it was his choice. Put up or shut up. Prove everyone wrong who thought he was a loser. The next week, he came to see me after school. He transferred to Sobriety High, worked with a therapist

on his anger issues and finally graduated last year." Alan grinned. "Now that I think about it, that was pretty stupid of me, wasn't it?"

"You got that right," I said. "If Mr. Lenzen had happened upon that little scene, he would have taken it out of your hide."

"Speaking of which, how's the sunburn, Red-man? Doesn't look too bad from here."

"Just don't charge me in the chest tomorrow morning when we play basketball, and I'll be fine."

"Hey, I don't charge, man. I play by the rules."

"That'll be the day," I muttered.

"So, I think you should come to the council meeting tonight and watch our boy in action," Alan said, abruptly changing the topic of conversation. "Karl's going to ask the council to delay voting on the proposal until after the bird survey."

"What time's the meeting? I've got softball after school."

"Not tonight, you don't. I can feel the rain moving in even as we speak, and it won't be letting up till tomorrow. Practice will be cancelled."

I gave him a suspicious look. "Don't tell me. Your wise old great-grandmother taught you how to sense a change in the weather?"

"Nope. CNN did. I had it on the television monitor in my classroom between periods. We've got a heck of a rain storm coming our way."

"Okay, so when's the meeting?"

"It starts at seven, but Karl won't be first on the agenda. I figure around 7:30 he'll be up."

If CNN was right and we got rained out after school, I could swing over to Chris's place by four o'clock to see how he was holding up, assuming he was still at home and not entertaining visitors at the county jail. Dani had left me instructions to his trailer last night before Mandy picked her up. She'd also promised to call Chris and tell him I'd be dropping in sometime today. I figured I'd give him a call when I was on my way there.

I also figured I could hit a double with my trip out to Chris's place, since the Northern Parula I wanted was in the Murphy-Hanrehan area, not far from Chris's trailer. As long as the rain wasn't

blowing in sheets, I could still see the warbler in the rain. Then, a quick stop for a burger for dinner, and I could make it to the council meeting in time for Karl's turn on the floor.

"I'll see what I can do," I told Alan.

The bell rang for third period.

"Gotta run," he said. "My public awaits. Or sleeps, as the case may be. Later, Red-man."

"Hey, Alan," I called just as he cleared the doorway.

He poked his head back in the office. "Yeah?"

"What do you think of Eric Stodegard?"

"Tough. Slick. Self-serving. Good at what he does—wheeling and dealing. I don't like the company he keeps—OEI to be exact. Why?"

"He's got a business proposition for Lily, but I have a bad feeling he's going to propose more than just business."

"You're worried about your sister."

I nodded.

"Look, Bob," Alan assured me. "I haven't seen your sister in . . . what? five or six years? . . . but as I recall, Lily is nobody's fool. Don't worry about the shrimp, Bob. She can handle herself."

"When it comes to business, yes. But when it comes to men, she seems to have a blind spot as big as Lake Minnetonka."

"So give her a paddle. She can use it to whomp on all the men you don't approve of."

"Like she'll really listen to what I think."

"You want me to talk to her? 'Hello Lily, you probably don't know me from Adam, but your brother thinks you're making a mistake with this guy. Of course, your brother thinks you make a mistake with every guy you date, but hey, what's a brother for anyway?' Give her time, Bob. Not even a smooth customer like Stodegard can hide what a jerk he is for very long. She'll figure it out."

He was probably right. I hoped he was.

So in the meantime, I just had to keep my mouth shut about Lily's choice of a potential business associate and/or romantic partner.

I knew my shins, at least, would thank me.

CHAPTER TWELVE

Sure enough, it started raining at noon. By three o'clock, all the sports practices were cancelled. At a quarter to four, I pulled up in front of Chris Olson's trailer. I parked next to an old pickup.

I sat in my car for a minute or two, listening to the rain drumming on the roof. What did I want to accomplish here? One—keep my promise to Dani to talk with her brother. Two—offer to help Chris locate resources to assist him in his legal situation if he didn't already know who to turn to. Three—there shouldn't be any "three," because if I did anything more than "one" and "two," then I was courting Mr. Lenzen's eternal wrath by getting involved in a murder investigation. Again.

But that water had long ago passed under this particular bridge. I may only have gotten my toes wet promising Dani to help her and Chris, but I was already preparing myself for a dive into the deep end. Someone had to look out for Dani's best interests and right now, I felt like I was the only candidate. Her mom had been murdered, her dad had casino fever, and her brother was the police's prime suspect. If any kid ever needed an advocate, it was Dani. So, after "one" and "two," I planned to go on to "three"—get Chris's side of the story, and "four"—either get him cleared or hooked up with the best legal help we could find. From what I'd gathered from Alan and Stodegard the Jerk, Chris needed an advocate even more than Dani did.

I dashed through the rain and knocked on the trailer door. Almost immediately, Chris opened it.

"I'm Mr. White, Dani's counselor at school," I said, offering him my hand to shake. "I called earlier."

"Yeah," he said and slammed his left fist into my jaw.

I staggered on his step.

"Keep your hands off my sister, you pervert."

Okay. Somebody miscommunicated here, and I was pretty sure it wasn't me. Especially since I wasn't saying a word because I was gingerly feeling the edge of my tongue in my mouth where I had accidentally bitten it when Chris Olson, defender of Dani's virtue, took a swing at me.

I put up both my hands in defense, ready to fend him off if he took another shot.

"Chris. I've never touched your sister. Ask her. She asked me to help you two. Go on—call her right now and ask her."

He looked at me standing there, rain sloping off my shoulders. He hesitated a moment, brushed his hand over his face and said, "You want to come in?"

"Yeah, as long as you're not going to hit me again."

He stepped aside to let me into the trailer. "Hey, I'm really sorry, Mr. White. It's just that the police told me that Dani said she spent the night with you, and I couldn't believe she'd lie to the police, so I figured there was some truth in it somewhere, and these last few days have been awful, and I don't know who to believe anymore." He closed the door behind me. "Are you all right? Did I hurt you?"

"Nah." I wiped a thread of blood off my lip with the side of my hand. My tongue felt swollen. I guessed I'd be sporting a bruise on my chin by morning. I'd be red, White, and blue. A regular American flag. Pin some stars on me and I could be in a parade.

"You got any ithe?" I asked Chris. I pointed to my chin. "It'th gonna thwell."

He crossed to his refrigerator in the tiny kitchen and pulled out a can of cold pop.

"Will this do?"

"Yeth."

I held it against my jaw and felt the cold radiate through my skin. It felt pretty good. At least the throbbing was letting up some. I eyed Chris over the edge of the can.

"Your sister," I finally managed to get out clearly, "has a habit of fabricating information to protect herself or the people she cares about. She didn't want anyone to get into trouble, so she made up the story about staying at my place the night your mother was murdered."

"But she didn't—" he started to protest, but I cut him off.

"Yeah, I know. Her intentions were good, but that doesn't undo the harm she did to me and to herself by lying to the police. Now they consider her unreliable, which isn't going to help either of you out here."

I brushed some damp hair off my forehead and took a quick survey of the trailer, still pressing the cold can against my jaw.

Neat. Orderly. Hand-me-down furniture. Clean. Nice digs for a nineteen-year-old guy.

A lot nicer than I had expected, to tell the truth. As far as I knew, most nineteen-year-olds weren't exactly Mr. Domestic. Their taste in décor usually ran more to leftover pizza boxes than to well-tended houseplants.

Which made me wonder—did Chris have a roommate of the female type?

"You keep a nice place, Chris," I commented. "Maybe you could give me some lessons. I'm kind of a slacker when it comes to housework."

He smiled a little and glanced around the living room. I noticed he had the same dark-brown hair as Dani and stood just a little shorter than I did. Where Dani was slim, however, Chris was built like a fullback. No wonder my jaw hurt. He didn't look like someone anyone would choose to pick a fight with, yet according to Dani, her mother had routinely bullied Chris until she finally tossed him out of the house.

"That's Dani, not me," Chris said, indicating the room with a shrug. "She's always picking up when she's here. Straightening things. Cleaning up. Arranging stuff so it looks nice. She's really good at making things look better than they are."

He caught my eye and seemed to want to say something else, but didn't.

"Do you want to sit down?" he asked, instead, nodding toward an old armchair.

I sat down on the edge of the seat cushion while he pulled over one of the two wooden chairs at the kitchen table.

"I told Dani I'd talk to you," I began to explain. "She's feeling pretty scared and confused and helpless right now, but she's more worried about you. Dani's a good kid, but even the best kids can only take so much. So I promised her I'd do what I could to help you out, but in all honesty, Chris, I'm not sure what that means at this point."

Especially in light of the fact that he'd just popped me one in the jaw, no questions asked. The kid acted first, thought later. Definitely not a good combination in any situation, but downright compromising when it came to being a suspect in a family homicide. What was I going to say when I had to make a character reference for him? He gave me a cold can to keep the bruise down after he punched me?

"I'm not a lawyer," I reminded him. "I'm not a police officer, and I'm not a member of the family. I'm Dani's school counselor. That's it."

"You're more than that, Mr. White," he insisted. "A lot more. You're someone she trusts, and Dani doesn't trust too many people. Believe me."

I knew that from personal experience. The first few weeks I'd worked with Dani had been a continual testing on her part, obviously a legacy of her dysfunctional relationship with her parents. She didn't trust adults, and I'd often had the feeling she was secretly gauging what to share with me and what to deliberately omit. Before her mother's murder, I'd been feeling pretty confident I'd made some inroads into her trust issues and that she was becoming more comfortable with confiding in me. I'd hoped she could extend that to other adults and begin building some positive relationships to help her navigate the years ahead. Now I wasn't so sure.

"Be that as it may," I told him, "I don't know that Dani's trust in me will be of much use to you, Chris."

I leaned forward and rested my forearms on my knees. "You're in serious trouble, here. You need to fully cooperate with the police."

"I know that. And I am cooperating."

I could see tears trying to form in his eyes, but he blinked them back.

"But I don't know what else to do, Mr. White. I didn't kill my mom. That's the truth. But I don't know how to make anyone else believe that. And in the meantime, Dani's got no one else. My dad's hopeless, Mr. White. He doesn't take care of her. He doesn't care about her at all. All he wants to do is gamble. All I want to do is give her a home, a real home. I was trying so hard. Keeping sober, staying out of trouble, meeting with my therapist. I was doing everything I had to do to get Dani turned over into my care as soon as I could take my parents to court and petition for Dani's custody. And now this . . ."

Chris put his face in his hands and started to cry. His broad shoulders shook with it. I reached out and touched his arm.

"Chris," I said. I held on to his arm while he cried, thinking again that he was just a kid, after all—a big kid with way too much on his personal plate. Clearly, he needed a lot more than I was equipped to give him. Right now, however, I could at least keep him company, and if he wanted to talk, I could sure listen.

That I could do.

"Chris," I said again, once his crying slowed down. "Tell me what happened on Saturday night. Maybe there's something you forgot to tell the police, something that would help you prove to them you're innocent. They haven't arrested you yet, which has to be a good sign. If they were sure that you were their man, I don't think you'd still be sitting here this afternoon."

I reminded myself that Rick had said "if" they were going to arrest Chris, it would be today. I hung on to that, along with mentally willing Detective Wilson to find another prime suspect as quickly as possible. Every minute that passed without the police at the door had to be in Chris's favor, I reasoned. Just how many minutes he would get, I had no idea, but I was determined to make the most of them.

"Think, Chris," I urged him. "Who else didn't get along with your mom? Did you ever see anything that might lead you to wonder about somebody? Did anyone come to the house while you were there? Whoever killed your mom knew where she lived and picked a time and place that no one else would be around. Who would know that stuff?"

Chris wiped his hand across his eyes. "Do you believe me?"

I believed he deserved an honest answer.

"I believe you need help," I said. "I believe your parents failed you and Dani. I don't want to think you killed your mom. But what I think or believe isn't going to get you out of this. What is going to get you out of this is giving the police every bit of information you can think of to help them solve your mom's murder. So," I said, settling back in the old armchair, "let's go over Friday night. Give me details, Chris. I'm really good with details."

At least I was when it came to identifying birds. Ask me what an immature Chestnut-sided Warbler looked like, and I could tell you in a heartbeat. Identifying clues that might lead to Nancy Olson's killer, though . . . well, I was pretty sure that was going to be another ball-game entirely.

Unfortunately, it looked like it was my turn at bat, so I stepped up to the plate and told Chris to give me his best pitch.

Chapter Thirteen

"It was Friday night," he began, "after supper."

His mother had shown up at his trailer unexpectedly, Chris said. She was looking for Dani because Dani hadn't come home after school. Furious with her daughter's disappearance, Nancy had accused Chris of turning Dani against her, and he'd laughed, saying she'd done it herself. They yelled insults at each other, and finally, Nancy Olson had threatened Chris, saying that if she found out that Dani had even stepped into his trailer in the last week, she would get a restraining order against him.

"As always, she knew just how to twist the knife." Chris said. "Dani had slipped up and told Mom I was planning to take them to court, so she was just itching to shoot me down. She knew that a restraining order would be all it'd take to screw up me and Dani permanently."

A muscle twitched in his jaw, and I could see the anger starting to simmer. Then he closed his eyes, took four huge deep breaths, and his face relaxed. He opened his eyes and smiled at me.

"A little trick I learned in my anger management classes," he explained. "I take a ten-second trip to the lake. It slows everything down for me, and then I can focus on the problem, not my feelings."

"Good for you," I said. I carefully touched my chilled cheek. "I wish you'd done that earlier, Chris. My jaw would have appreciated it."

"Right." Chris nodded, then shook his head. "I'm such an idiot."

"Happens to the best of us."

"Then my mom left," Chris finished. "I stayed home all night, watching television. It was pouring rain, so I didn't want to go out. The next day the cops showed up in the afternoon and took me in for questioning. That's all, Mr. White."

"Nobody stopped by, called . . . anything that would give you an alibi?"

He was silent for a minute, staring at the floor. He took another deep breath.

"No."

I didn't know Chris, but my counselor's gut instinct instantly kicked in: he was lying.

"Chris, are you sure? Absolutely sure?"

He shifted on the chair.

My gut kicked again.

"Chris, is there something you're not saying?"

He wouldn't meet my eyes. He seemed to be thinking it over. After a moment or two, he finally lifted his head and looked at me.

"Someone did stop by. But it was earlier, before my mom came over."

"And?"

"I didn't want to say anything about it because it only makes me look worse." He waited a couple beats before taking a deep breath and continuing.

"It was this guy Eric Stodegard. He's a realtor. He'd been calling me up for weeks, promising me a good job with his real estate office if I'd convince my mom to vote for the development proposal for the old Dandorff farm. You heard about that? I'd been telling him 'no,' because my mom and I . . . well, you know . . . we can't—couldn't—be in the same room without . . ."

He shook his head and quickly wiped his hand across his eyes again.

"But I got to thinking that maybe I could say something to her, something that might at least make her think about it, and if I had a good job with Stodegard, it would really help my case to get Dani, so I told Stodegard to stop by and we'd talk. I thought, for Dani, I'd do anything."

Eric Stodegard.

My, my.

OEI's point man was wheeling and dealing with a nineteen-year-old?

I recalled what Lily had said at dinner on Sunday about Stodegard's claim that the property development proposal was in the bag. Had Stodegard been betting that Chris could sway Nancy Olson? If so, the man had seriously underestimated the strength of that familial bond.

But then I remembered what the snake had said at the coffee shop this morning. Everyone on the council knew about Nancy's problems with Chris, which meant that Stodegard couldn't have thought he'd gain some advantage from that angle. In fact, based on what he'd said at Joy of Java, Stodegard had no use at all for Chris.

Or at least, he didn't now.

But according to Chris, Stodegard had been badgering him for help. Now, I had to ask myself: Why would a high-powered realtor like Stodegard go to a kid with a record of assault and drinking, a kid who lived in a trailer because his mother had kicked him out of the family home?

Especially when everyone knew the mother and son had a volatile relationship.

"Chris," I said, trying to keep my voice evenly pitched, so I wouldn't prejudice his answer. "Did he ever ask you to hurt your mom?"

"No."

I let out a breath I hadn't realized I was holding. Okay, so maybe I was letting my suspicious imagination run away with me. The guy

just hadn't scored any points with me over coffee. Didn't mean he was a total low-life.

"At least," Chris added, softly, "not in those words. I mean, he didn't ask me to beat her up or anything like that. I got the idea that he wanted me to pressure her to vote for his project and that maybe if she wouldn't listen to me, it wouldn't be good for her. You know? Like he was going to spread it around about our family. My dad's gambling, my police record, stuff like that."

Ah, yes. Slander. A time-honored political strategy.

That did merit points for Stodegard, I decided.

Points in the "loser" column.

At the same time, though, I had to give him credit—he'd known exactly where he could hurt Nancy Olson the most. From what Dani had told me in our counseling sessions, her mother the councilwoman was obsessed with her public image as a leader in the community. The possibility of parading her family's multiple dysfunctions for public review would have been her worst nightmare; it certainly would have cost her her seat on the council in the next election, along with any political ambitions she might have harbored for the future. By sending his threat to her by way of Chris, Stodegard also neatly protected his own back: not only would he have initiated the emotional blackmail that might have secured him Nancy's vote, but she wouldn't even know who the real enemy was.

"But when he got here, I just couldn't do it," Chris said, stopping my train of thought in its tracks. "He showed up, and I told him 'no.' I don't care what it would have done to my mom, but there's no way I'd want Dani in the center of that circus. The local media would eat her alive. So I told him to take the job and shove it. I'll find some other job somewhere."

Thank goodness. Chris, at least, had his priorities in the right place when it came to Dani. Unlike the rest of his family.

"You're a good man, Chris," I told him. "What did the police say when you told them about Stodegard?"

He looked down at the floor again.

"You did tell them, didn't you?"

He shook his head.

Even as the question formed on my lips, I knew his answer. It would make him look even worse as a suspect. Stodegard's offer of employment could be considered a prime motive for murder. The last thing Chris wanted was for the police to know about it and its very specific conditions.

"I figured he'd deny it all, Mr. White," Chris said, misery weighing down his every word. "He said to forget I'd ever met him, that he didn't need me anyway. Then he left."

"That's it?"

"That's it."

I decided I needed some time to sift through the things Chris had told me. I understood his reluctance to tell the police about his connection with Stodegard, but I couldn't convince him that it would be a good move to call Wilson and repeat the information. For one thing, since Chris hadn't been forthcoming with it in his first interview with the police, it sounded too much now like a calculated change in his story. Dani's credibility, thanks to her little fiction about our private pajama party, was already shot with the police. Jeopardizing Chris's credibility with a delayed addendum wasn't going to help matters.

I checked my watch. It was only five o'clock, which gave me plenty of time to look for the Parula, which was good, since looking for it would calm me down considerably, and I wanted a shot at finding it before the council meeting.

Yeah, some birding would be a very good idea, I realized. Hopefully, it would give me a chance to clear my head, too, figure out a way to help Chris, and prevent me from taking a shot at something else: Eric Stodegard.

I mean, really. What kind of snake—no, worse than a snake—scum—would bribe a kid to blackmail his own mother?

Can you spell "Stodegard"?

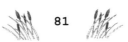

I thought you could.

I knew I could.

I could also spell "trouble," with a capital T.

Make that "double trouble": the scum was planning to spend time with my sister.

"Nice and slow" time.

Not if I could help it. Man the torpedoes, Mr. White.

"I'll be in touch," I told Chris and trotted to my car. Minutes later I parked at one of the trailheads in Murphy-Hanrehan, where the Parula had been reported. The rain had slacked off some, so I pulled out the rain poncho I keep behind my seat and got out to hike up the trail.

As I walked, I tried to sort out my impressions of Chris.

First and foremost, it was obvious he was devoted to his sister. How many nineteen-year-olds could suck up their own shortcomings and work towards redemption just so they could take on the responsibility of caring for a dependent sibling? Chris had kicked alcohol, finished high school and even taken anger management classes to make himself a better candidate for becoming his sister's guardian. Pretty impressive for a kid who was frequently in trouble with the cops just four years ago.

He'd also opted to take the legal route to gaining custody of his sister. That showed planning, patience, and maturity—not the most typical traits of young men pushing twenty years old.

And, of course, lest I forget, Chris did have a heck of a left hook, too.

I flexed my jaw. Yeah, I'd learned that first-hand.

The good news was that I'd also learned that Dani's brother was a lousy liar.

Thanks to years of watching kids squirm all over the place in my office at school, body language is an open book for me, and Chris's spoke volumes. Every time he'd fidgeted or refused to make eye contact, red flags were flying in my head that he was hiding something. It also told me he wasn't skilled at deception. The accomplished liars I

had met over the years didn't bat an eye when they told a lie because, to them, it wasn't a lie, it was their version of the truth. Chris, on the other hand, couldn't even look in my direction, let alone in my eye, when he was hiding something. As a result, I was pretty convinced now that he was telling the truth when he said he hadn't killed his mother. At the same time, however, there seemed to be things hovering in the air that he wouldn't put into words.

Something about Dani and her need to arrange things to look nice.

Something about Friday night.

I scanned the trees near the trail and saw several Palm Warblers flitting through the branches. After listening for a few seconds, I picked up the *see-weet see-weet, see-weet* song of a Nashville Warbler, and then, another hundred yards around the crest of the hill, I heard the Northern Parula's rising buzzy trill. This was too easy, I thought. It was almost exactly where the list serve had said it was.

And then, there it was.

Even in the drizzle, the Parula was brilliant. Its bright yellow throat and breast were almost a tiny beacon in the rain, its gray-blue back topped by a yellowish-green patch. Two white bars marked each wing, while across the chest, reddish and black bands identified the bird as a male. His white belly and the white rim that circled his eyes completed the picture, and not for the first time, I marveled at the infinite variety of coloration displayed by warblers.

Like I already said, I'm into details. I didn't spend years memorizing bird field guides for nothing, you know. When I see a bird, I want to be sure I know what I'm seeing. Name, rank, and species.

Too bad Chris's situation wasn't equally clear-cut. It seemed like the more he told me, the muddier the water got. I had known from Rick that Nancy Olson had gone to Chris's on Saturday night, but I didn't know she had threatened him with a restraining order. I also now knew the plan Chris had to get Dani out of the Olson home: a court hearing.

And Chris wasn't about to mess that up with a fight with his mom.

Yet he'd also told me he'd do anything for Dani.

And then Eric Stodegard had turned up in the mix.

Gee, I could hardly wait to see what else popped up in this mess. I turned around to go back to the car and stopped in my tracks.

Talk about surprises.

A Pine Warbler was sitting on a branch almost in front of my face. Unlike the short-tailed Parula, the Pine has a long tail, as well as a relatively large bill; its greenish-olive feathers and dark-streaked yellow breast almost make it disappear amidst spring leaves. For a split-second, it froze on the branch before flying off—I didn't know which of us was more surprised at the presence of the other. I made a mental note to myself to post it when I got home later after the council meeting.

Two for one, I could say. Come for the Parula and stay for the Pine.

I definitely needed to get out of the rain.

Unfortunately, that wasn't going to happen right away.

Even as I approached my SUV, I could tell something wasn't right.

It looked . . . shorter.

I glanced at the tires.

All flat.

I heard a whistle.

Not a warbler.

A bullet.

I dove behind the car.

CHAPTER FOURTEEN

Crap, crap, crap.

With my face in the mud, I could hear a car engine gun and race away. I slowly lifted my head and peered through the drizzle, but I was alone in the trailhead parking lot. I hoisted myself up, looked around and brushed off the damp earth that was clinging to my poncho.

"Since when did birding have to get so dangerous?" I complained to the great outdoors, which, right now, didn't seem so great to me.

I climbed into the car and dialed 911. About three minutes later, a squad car pulled up behind me.

"Man, I can't leave you alone for twenty-four hours."

It was Rick.

I pushed open the passenger door, and he got in. "What are you doing here? I thought you were the school cop."

"I am," he replied. "I also just happened to be in the vicinity when I heard the dispatcher with your report. Figured I'd come check it out."

"You were doing a little birding on your break, weren't you? Right here in Murphy-Hanrehan."

He put up his hands in mock surrender. "I take the fifth."

"Find anything?"

"Yeah," he said. "Got a Pine near the other trailhead, and I thought I heard a Hooded Warbler, but that's when my radio went off. I figure we can go back and look if you want. With four flats, you're not going anywhere anyway." He glanced at a streak of mud on my poncho. "Birding from the horizontal?"

"Somebody took a shot at me. I dove for cover."

Rick's face went serious. "You're sure?"

"Yeah, I'm sure. I dove for cover. How do you think I got mud smeared on my jacket?"

"No," Rick said. "I mean, you're sure someone was shooting at you? You're sure it was you someone was aiming at and not your tires? I'm betting we find bullets are the cause of the flats."

"Why? Has there been a run of shot-out tires here at the park?"

"Not lately," he admitted. "Kids get kinda crazy in the spring. We start getting reports of vandalism once the weather turns nice."

Yeah, I knew how spring affected kids. I saw it in my office almost non-stop the last two months of school every year: students sent to see me for picking fights in the parking lot, painting their class years on the football field, skipping school to drive to Wisconsin to buy fireworks. So far, though, no one had been referred to me for shooting at a counselor in a public park.

There's always a first time for everything, right?

"Rick, all four tires were already flat when I approached the car. Let's say they were shot out by some kid. Why fire a fifth bullet? To shoot out my spare?"

Rick rubbed his ear stud and frowned. "Not good," he said.

"Tell me about it."

He sat back against the seat and stared out the windshield at the rain trickling across the glass. "Did you tick anybody off today? More than usual, I mean."

"Very funny. No, I didn't give anyone a really good reason to follow me out here and try to gun me down. Besides, I didn't come straight here from school. I stopped at Chris Olson's trailer to talk with him about what's going on. He told me he's been planning to take his folks to court and try to get custody of Dani."

"Oh yeah?" Rick's fingers drummed the top of the service revolver holstered at his waist. "Good for him. And Dani. They've got a plan."

"A plan that won't do either of them any good if he's arrested for his mother's murder."

"It's not going to happen. At least, not right now," Rick added. "Wilson's convinced there might be strong motives for murder floating around on the county council. He's got a couple officers investigating, so until he rules out suspects in that corner, he'll wait on bringing Chris in."

What a relief. Chris had a reprieve. I couldn't wait to tell Dani. "But our little crime scene here," Rick said, tapping the seat beside his leg, "this is a problem because either someone was shooting at you for a reason, or someone was shooting at you for no reason. Either way, we've got a shooter loose." His fingers went back to tapping on the top of his pistol. "And, either way, it's not going to help Chris."

"What do you mean?"

"You know how I said we hadn't had a run of shot-out tires lately?"

"Yeah." I suddenly got a bad feeling I wasn't going to like the direction this conversation was taking.

"Well, we haven't. Not since about four years ago. Not since Chris Olson cleaned up his act."

Great. Now I knew I wasn't going to like the direction of this conversation. "You want to spell this out for me?"

Rick's fingers stilled on the butt of his pistol. "Chris Olson was hell on wheels for a while, Bob. Four years ago, we had tires shot out in this parking lot every weekend. We finally caught the vandal in the act."

I looked away from Rick and out my side window.

"It was Chris. When I file this report, it's going to look bad for him, Bob. Worse than bad. Not only do I have four shot-out tires, I've got an attempted shooting on my hands."

And we were barely ten minutes from Chris's trailer. Where I'd spent an hour trying to help him find a way out of being a murder suspect after he nailed me with a left hook.

What kind of sap was I, anyway?

"Anybody know you were in this area?"

I looked back at Rick.

"Chris."

"Shit."

He got that right.

CHAPTER FIFTEEN

Did I miss anything?"

I slipped into the seat next to Alan. After Rick and I made a quick search for the Hooded Warbler—we didn't find it—he'd driven me into town and dropped me off at the council chambers. I'd taken off my muddy poncho and left it on the coat rack in the front hall. Rick promised to get a tow truck out to Murphy-Hanrehan to retrieve my car and get some new tires put on. I glanced down the row past Alan and saw Karl, and beside him, Bridget.

"Bridget?" I whispered to Alan.

"Yup." His eyes never strayed from the face of Arne Bjorkland, the county council member who was summarizing the development proposal for Dandorff's property. "The temperature has been steadily rising in here ever since they sat down next to each other. I'm getting heat rash just being in the same room with them. Spring fever has sprung."

"Tell me something I don't know," I muttered back. Bridget could do worse, I figured. A lot worse. Karl was a great kid. Outgoing, motivated, friendly. I stole a quick glance in her direction. Hmm. Her wardrobe wasn't quite up to first lady standards yet, though. She'd have to kiss her tank tops and short shorts goodbye. The wife of the president of the United States couldn't show up in public with her belly button showing. Maybe at the game tomorrow I'd give her some clothing guidelines. Forewarned is forearmed.

Or at least better dressed.

Speaking of which, the best-dressed man in the room was walking up to the easel that had been set in front of the council's worktable. I couldn't help but notice that Stodegard had on another perfectly tailored, very expensive suit. I almost expected him to do a model's turn at the front of the room.

"The council appreciates your being here tonight, Eric," Arne said. "I think you probably have a few things to add to my summary."

"Yes, I do, Arne. And I appreciate the opportunity to do that tonight. As all the council members know, OEI has invested an enormous amount of time and effort into developing their whole-site business plan. At the same time, they have listened earnestly to the concerns of local residents about environmental impact and quality of life."

He flipped a page on the easel to reveal an artist's rendering of the schematics of the OEI site plan.

"Very colorful," I whispered to Alan. "I like how they shaded all the parking lots in different shades of grey. Kind of makes you forget that all that space is currently bright green."

He elbowed me in the ribs.

"The outdoor amphitheater you see here," Stodegard pointed to another drawing, "will have state-of-the-art acoustic features to guarantee the integrity of the musical performances. Whether a concertgoer sits in the first row or the fiftieth, their musical experience will be consistently outstanding."

"Assuming they want to hear screaming amplifiers instead of birds singing," I added under my breath.

I took another shot in my ribs.

Geez. My jaw ached, I'd rolled in the mud, missed a bullet, and now my best friend was beating me up. And to put the icing on my cake of misery, I now had to be a polite audience for Stodegard the Scum.

Try a little objectivity here, Bob, I told myself. I mean, what did I really know about the guy, except that he was an insensitive jerk, had

tried to bribe a kid, attempted to exploit a dysfunctional family, plotted at least political harm to a council person, was playing my sister with a financial contract (and that had better be the only thing he was playing with), and had been to lunch with the woman I intended to marry.

Hoped to marry.

After I asked her.

Which I was going to do soon.

I hoped.

"Down, boy," Alan whispered, leaning sideways towards me.

I looked at him in surprise. "What?"

"You are giving off waves of tension that even I can feel," Alan said in a barely audible voice. "Tell me about it later. Right now, you listen."

Stodegard, who, by the way, was still definitely a scum, finished his presentation and sat down. At that point, the council members started making comments on the proposal. Arne, a birder long before I was born, was unabashedly opposed to the proposal, while Sharon Claver, the only woman—now—on the council, was adamantly pro-development, citing the need for the county to increase revenues to improve various services to its growing number of constituents. Sitting on the fence were Kevin Ray, the fellow who Bridget had said was her grandpa's friend and neighbor, and Janssen, Savage High's sports booster cheerleader.

I took another look at Janssen. Without his Go Bass hat, I almost didn't recognize him.

Arne introduced Karl to the group then, and Karl stood up to ask the council to delay taking a vote on the proposal until after the birding survey on Thursday evening. He explained that the survey could yield valuable information that the council members would want to consider before they made a decision that would have such a long-term impact on the community, as well as the environment.

"Nice verbiage," I noted to Alan.

"It better be," he agreed. "I coached him most of the afternoon."

Two rows in front of us, Stodegard stood up.

"With all due respect," he objected, "a delay at this point could be disastrous for any kind of working relationship we hope to establish with OEI. My client has been more than patient with the six months of review and deliberation this council has already devoted to the proposal. I know, for a fact, that OEI has been scouting other locations for their complex and that they are prepared to drop this project entirely in order to pursue other options if the council doesn't come to an agreement by the end of this week."

The four council members exchanged glances of concern.

"I urge you not to let this tremendous opportunity for the county slide away," Stodegard practically demanded. "My client needs an answer now. Delaying that answer is a mistake. We all stand to lose in that case."

Oh, yeah? I wondered just how much Stodegard himself stood to lose. Thousands in commission? Tens of thousands?

"I hear what you're saying, Mr. Stodegard," Arne said, "but I can't in good conscience ignore pertinent information we have yet to consider. If my fellow council members are agreeable, I move we meet in special session on Friday afternoon to take our vote. If Mr. Solvang can have his survey results to us at that time, we can review them and make our decision before OEI's deadline."

"I can do that," Karl assured him.

"With all due respect," Stodegard began again, but was cut off by Janssen.

"I second the motion," Janssen said. "I'd like to thank Karl for his initiative and hard work on this. His concern for the legacy we will leave future generations is both admirable and thought-provoking. I know that I will certainly review those survey results carefully and critically."

The motion was approved unanimously, and then the meeting was adjourned. Stodegard didn't look happy. In fact, I thought he looked downright venomous.

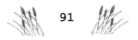

Okay, not a scum. He was back to being a snake.

"Nice work, Karl," I said, standing up to shake his hand. "It sounds like you're making a mark on this decision." I smiled at my ballplayer. "Bridget, I didn't know you were interested in local government."

Bridget blushed just a little before taking a quick look at Karl. It was more than obvious which part of the local government she was interested in.

"Since our practice was cancelled this afternoon, I thought I'd come tonight to see what a council meeting was like, Mr. White," Bridget explained. "Karl's been telling me about the citizen's group, and I think it's really great that he cares so much about what's going on in the community."

She threw Karl another warm glance.

"Besides," she added, "I want to know what's going to happen to my grandpa's farm."

I turned to our future president. "Karl, your grandparents live out in that area, too, don't they?"

"They live a couple miles down the road from Mr. Dandorff," he said. "But they're the reason I got interested in this whole thing. They've got a beautiful place, but if OEI builds their complex, it just won't be the same anymore. There'll be traffic, noise, and a lot more lights out there, especially at night. All those parking lot lights and marquees they want to put in will block out all the stars you see now. On a clear night, you can see a million stars from my grandparents' farm. I'd hate to seen that gone."

"But you'd get to see stars of another kind, Karl. Celebrities. Musicians. Performing artists. Big names."

I turned to find Stodegard behind me. "Big deal," I said.

CHAPTER SIXTEEN

I t's a huge deal," the realtor corrected me.

He must have slithered up behind us while I was talking with Bridget.

"That's why there's so much at stake here for the community," he insisted. "It's not just about money. It's about community pride and topnotch amenities."

Yeah, right.

It was about money.

Stodegard shook Karl's hand in congratulations. "Very nice presentation, Karl. I'm impressed. You have a lot of confidence for a high school senior. You're the kind of young person we like to see getting involved in our community's future."

"Thank you," Karl said. "But we're on opposite sides in this case, Mr. Stodegard. I'm hoping to provide the council with enough information to convince them to refuse OEI's proposal. When I come back to the council with the results on Friday, I'm hoping we'll get a victory for native preservation."

"Just might happen," Ray commented, coming up to clap Karl on the shoulder. "Good job, Karl. Maybe too good. You're scaring the opposition." He winked and nodded toward Stodegard.

"Don't get me wrong," Stodegard insisted. "I'm all for conservation. We've got some nice tracts of land already in reserve around the area which I think will easily meet our needs for open spaces and habitat. But

Dandorff's property, developed by OEI, would be a boon to the community's future. The trade-off of unused land for increased revenue —"

"Oh, give it a rest, Eric," Ray interrupted. "We've all heard it. Let's talk about the Bass's chance of winning one this season. How about it, Bridget?"

Bridget blushed again.

I extended my hand to Ray. "I'm Bob White, a counselor at Savage. I'm also one of the coaches for the Bass."

"And a darn good batting coach, I understand." Fritz Dandorff was standing next to Bridget, his arm clasped around her shoulders. "Bridget's been telling me about how hard you're working her. I expect to see some good hits in that game tomorrow night."

"Oh, Grandpa, are you going to come?" Bridget was clearly pleased.

"You bet. Kevin says he'll drive me, since my night vision is so poor. I don't get around the way I used to, you know."

You'd never guess it from looking at Fritz Dandorff. Still spry and pink-cheeked, the old farmer must have been close to eighty years old with a full head of white hair. It didn't take much to imagine him hopping up on a tractor or stalking the north forty checking the fields. His weathered hands were sure and steady on Bridget's shoulders and his eyes sharp and clear. He reminded me of an old Peregrine Falcon, tough and quick and focused.

"But the game's early, Grandpa. Right after school," Bridget reminded him. "It won't be dark even by the time we're done."

"Well, I'll still let Kevin tag along. He likes driving that old classic of mine."

He looked up to see that Ray was out of hearing, having walked across the room to speak with Janssen.

"He gets pretty lonesome now, since his wife passed away," he confided. He gave Bridget's shoulder a squeeze. "Me, I've still got you and your brothers and your folks for company, but old Kevin's all alone. Besides," he grinned, "I've got to have somebody to brag to when you hit those home runs."

We talked a little bit more about the Bass and our opponents tomorrow night. Then, as the conversation wound down, I couldn't help but wonder what had happened all those years ago to dissuade Bridget's grandfather from turning his property into park land. I knew it might be rude and even intrusive, but if anyone had the answer to that question, it was Dandorff himself. I thought briefly of Dani and all the times I had encouraged her to be more vocal about her needs and wants. I figured it was time to take some of my own advice.

Imagine that.

"I've got to ask," I said to Dandorff. "Wasn't there some discussion a few years ago that you were going to donate your land for a preserve?"

Bridget looked stricken and glanced quickly at her grandfather. The old farmer's face had frozen, and I thought, okay, rude and intrusive may not be such a good idea here.

How do I back out of this one?

Karl, prospective leader of the free world—God bless America—came to my rescue.

"That was a hard time, wasn't it, Mr. Dandorff?" Karl nodded at the old man. "I remember all the neighbors in town—heck, I think it was the whole Minnesota River Valley—came to Mrs. Dandorff's funeral. We even had folks staying out at my grandparents' farm because all the motels were full. Everybody loved Mrs. D. My grandma says this county just isn't the same since she passed away."

Dandorff's face had, thankfully, thawed while Karl was speaking.

"No," Dandorff agreed quietly. "It's just not the same."

Totally embarrassed, I opened my mouth to apologize for reminding him of painful memories, when he cut me off with a kindness I was sure I didn't deserve at the moment.

"It's okay, Coach. You didn't know. But that's the answer to your question. After Millie died, I didn't think I could stand to see the farm remain the way it was—even as a park. Because it's not the way it was. Not anymore."

Dandorff gave Bridget's shoulder a final squeeze. "And, besides, I want to put these grandkids through college. If OEI buys the land, these kids can go wherever they want. And me, well, it's time for a fresh start. I'm thinking about traveling and maybe one of those luxury condos somewhere. Without Millie, I don't want to stay on the farm. OEI's money can make a lot of things happen, Coach."

He gave Bridget a big smacking kiss on the cheek and left us to join Ray across the room with the other council members.

As I watched him greet Arne and Janssen, it was clear to me that Fritz Dandorff had a lot to gain if OEI bought his property and a lot to lose if they didn't. Ray was his longtime good friend. When the time came for the proposal vote, would Ray vote yes as a favor to his friend, no matter what? In the discussion during the meeting, he'd seemed reluctant to state his opinions. I could only assume that meant he was still weighing the pros and cons of the project. Either that, or he didn't want to alienate anyone in the room by announcing a decision he had already made—a decision that would assuredly ruffle the feathers of at least a few of his council colleagues, not to mention his constituents who, according to Karl and Alan, appeared to be pretty evenly spread on both sides of the issue.

I asked Alan for a ride home, and we headed out of the chambers to retrieve my poncho. For the first time, he took a good look at me.

"What happened to you?"

"I thought you'd never ask," I replied.

"You've got a bruise on your jaw."

"It matches the one in my ribs, thanks to you."

"Are you going to tell me or do I have to play twenty questions?"

"That was your first one. Only nineteen to go."

"Smart ass."

"Let's get in the car. I'll tell you on the way home."

Alan popped the lock on his new hybrid parked at the far end of the lot. I slid into the passenger seat and dropped my poncho at my feet. The car still had that new car smell. The dash had more indicators and gauges than an airplane cockpit. The CD player held six discs.

"Nice," I told him. I thought about what Dani had said about Mandy. "If you were my best friend, you'd loan me this car."

Alan laughed and pushed the ignition button. The car's electric engine started without a sound. "No, I wouldn't. You've got your own car. Speaking of which, where is it?"

"Now, this is an interesting story," I told him, and I proceeded to give him the play-by-play of my visit to Chris and my mud-sliding at Murphy-Hanrehan and my rescue from wheellessness by Rick. The hybrid's engine was so quiet and the ride so smooth, it was hard to believe we were even moving, but by the time I finished my tale, Alan was pulling into my driveway.

"Geez Louise, White-man," Alan said, turning off the car with another touch to the ignition button. "You sure find things to do when a softball practice gets cancelled."

"So, what do you think, Alan?" I asked him. "Either Chris is an incredibly troubled young man and an exceptionally skilled liar who decided to make me and my car target practice after he snowed me with his innocence, or someone else is taking pot shots at me. Quite frankly, I'm not especially fond of either possibility."

Alan let out a sigh and gripped his hands high on the steering wheel. "You're not going to like this, but here's what I think. My gut tells me that Chris did not kill his mother, and he did not shoot out your tires or take a shot at you. Which means someone else did."

He paused, and I waited for him to spit out the rest.

"And since that someone who went after your tires stayed around to shoot at you, but didn't even nick you with the bullet, my guess is that the someone wanted to give you a message." He slid a glance at me. "You didn't make anyone really angry at you today, right?"

I snorted. "You sound like Rick. What is it with you guys? Do I have a reputation for making people angry or something? Me? Mr. Sensitive, Tissue King, High School Counselor? No, I didn't make anyone angry."

"Okay, then. That leaves one rather obvious conclusion. The someone who shot at you didn't like you being in the area."

"I was birding, Alan, not trespassing on private property. Even if I had been doing that, I'm pretty sure it's still not legal to shoot trespassers on sight. I think Savage is a little more civilized than that. And besides, no one knew I was going to be there. I went straight to the park after seeing Chris."

"I know," he said. "This is the part you're really not going to like."

"I thought you said that your gut says Chris wasn't my shooter."

"He wasn't," Alan repeated. "What I'm saying is that someone is trying to scare you away from Chris. Someone saw you at the trailer, followed you to the park, vandalized the car and took a shot at you to make trouble for Chris because someone knew that Chris would be the obvious suspect. And the last thing Chris needs right now is more trouble with the law, not to mention being blamed for a random shooting."

I stared out the windshield. "You're saying that someone is trying to frame Chris for Nancy's murder." I turned back to Alan. "And that the person who sent a bullet at me today might well be Nancy's murderer."

Alan looked grim. "Yeah, that's what I'm saying, Bob."

"And that murderer might not be averse to killing somebody else—somebody who tries to help Chris."

"Maybe."

Alan was right. I really didn't like this part.

"So, White-man, what you need to do is stay away from Chris Olson until Wilson makes an arrest."

I thought about my promise to Dani to help her and Chris out and my promise to myself not to let her down. "I don't think I can do that, Alan."

He nodded. "Yeah, that's what I figured you'd say. So at least don't go out to Chris's trailer again, okay? Have him come see you at school. It's safer. For both of you."

I could only hope Alan was right.

CHAPTER SEVENTEEN

I snagged the ball as it bounced off the basket rim and took it to the top of the key. Rick was all over me, trying to block my shot. Alan was still standing to the far left of the basket where he'd taken his missed shot, his hands on his hips, shaking his head.

"What's up with you, Hawk?" I panted, pivoting, keeping Rick dancing around me. "I don't think I've ever seen you miss that shot twice in a row."

Rick grabbed the ball out of my hands and drove for the basket. I reached him just as he went up to shoot. The ball swished through the net.

"Pretty," I said.

Outside, the sun was already shining when I'd arrived for our weekly before-school basketball game. I'd survived the night in my town house uneventfully, which meant no one had shown up to shoot me, accuse me of child molestation, or arrest me for being an idiot. All in all, it had been a good night.

Before we'd started the game, I'd left the gym doors open to let in some of the fresh morning air, but after thirty minutes of hard play, the smell of sweat was hanging thick on the court. My shirt was wet, sticking to my back and chest, and I swiped my forehead to keep the sweat out of my eyes. Yesterday's rain had left the air humid; even inside the cavernous gym, the dew point was rising. I joined Alan and Rick off the court, where they were draining water bottles.

"The home court is going to be the home lake if this humidity keeps up," I said.

"We are the Bass, Bob," Rick pointed out. "What do you expect?"

"Air conditioning, maybe?" I turned to Alan. "Are you sick or what? I haven't seen your game this bad since . . . ever."

He shrugged his shoulders and took another slug of water. "Guess I'm entitled to one off day, don't you think?"

Now I knew he was sick. Alan was the most competitive man I'd ever met, for crying out loud. Granted, he masked it with a very laid-back, easy-going façade, but I'd known Alan for more than sixteen years. I roomed with him in college when he was a star athlete and made mincemeat of every opponent he faced on the basketball court. I saw him burn the midnight oil more than once to ace exams because getting the second-best grade in the class wasn't good enough. And I don't call him Hawk just because it's short for Thunderhawk—he's Hawk because he's got the classic attributes of a predator: he's sharp, quick, strong, and he rarely misses his objective.

An off day?

Not in this lifetime.

But he sure wasn't offering any information at this point, either. Come to think of it, he hadn't said much while we played this morning. He was usually the one doing all the chatter, trying to distract me and Rick while he ran circles around us on the court. I made a mental note to check with him later in the day. Something was up with him. Maybe he'd be more talkative when Rick wasn't around.

Besides, right now, I was more interested in finding out what Rick had to say about our little crime scene last night. After Alan had dropped me off at home following the council meeting, I'd found my car parked in the garage, four new tires on the wheels, with a big IOU note from Rick taped to the windshield along with my keys.

"So here's the scoop, gentlemen," Rick said, tossing his empty bottle into the recycle bin by the gym door. "I got our ballistics guy to look at the bullets I had the mechanic dig out of your tires, Bob, and guess what? They're a perfect match with the bullet from Nancy Olson's chest. Now doesn't that just make you feel special?" he asked me.

"Special" wasn't quite the word I had in mind.

"Screwed" would have been closer.

"To be honest with you, Rick, that's kind of the conclusion Alan and I came to last night," I confessed. "We figured my shooting was somehow connected to Nancy's."

"The good news, though," he continued, "is that they're not a match for the bullets Chris Olson used to put in tires four years ago. And before you ask, yes, Chris has a gun registered to him, but we already know it's not the gun that killed Nancy. That doesn't mean Chris is off the radar, by any means, but it's enough to make Wilson wonder why someone else would try to make it look like Chris was back at tire-shooting. Along with some other things," he added.

"Like what?" Alan asked.

"You didn't hear it from me," Rick said, "but there are some questions about Pete Olson's alibi. That, and the fact that he seems to have come into a chunk of money. A rather big chunk of money."

Pete Olson.

Dani's dad.

In all my focus on wanting Chris to not be his mother's murderer, I'd just about forgotten about his father. I remembered Dani telling me that her dad had just bought her a new bed. What had she said? Oh yeah—that he was on a winning streak at the casino.

"Dani told me that he won big at the casino," I said.

Rick shook his head. "Wilson checked with the manager at Little Six. They haven't had a big winner in weeks. The dealers at the black-jack tables all know Olson. Nobody's seen him win more than he loses. Ever. On top of that, the dealer that backed up Olson's alibi for Friday night is waffling now. It was a busy night, and she can't be positive he was there the whole time."

"Where did you hear Olson had money?" Alan asked.

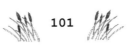

"You didn't hear this from me, either," Rick reminded us. "After Wilson talked with Dandorff the other night, thanks to Bob's tip from Bridget, he's had investigators quietly checking out not only the OEI guy—Stodegard—but the other county council members as well. Turns out, Kevin Ray visits Little Six on a fairly regular basis, too. He's gambled with Pete. And Pete has got major, major debts. Or at least he did until Monday night."

"What happened Monday night?"

"Pete showed up at Little Six with big ones in his pocket, according to Ray. Told Ray his money troubles were over."

"Pete Olson is a fool," Alan said, a hint of anger in his voice, "but I guess we already knew that. Still. Flashing money days after his wife's death? What's he thinking—that no one will notice? They haven't even had the funeral yet." He pulled his arm back and sent his empty water bottle sailing up over his head on a perfect trajectory to the recycling bin. "At least he could show some respect and stay out of the casinos a couple nights for Dani's sake."

"Nice shot." Alan was having no problems with his concentration now, I noticed. Over the years, I'd learned that anger had a way of doing that for some people. Fueled by a hot rush of adrenaline, their focus sharpened, their aim improved and their strength doubled.

Hmm. Maybe I should try getting my softball players mad. Nothing else seemed to be working.

"You haven't even heard the most interesting part of it," Rick continued. "A couple weeks ago, Pete told Ray some guy had approached him at the blackjack table and offered him money to convince Nancy to support the OEI deal."

"You have got to be kidding," I said.

"Nope. Of course, Pete told the guy to get lost, but now, you've got to wonder . . ." Rick headed for the locker room. "And that, my friends, is why Pete Olson has shot—pardon the pun—to near the top of the suspect list. Whether he's the one who was at our crime scene yesterday afternoon, too, Bob, well, that's up for grabs."

"Near the top," I repeated. "Does that mean there's someone else in the number one spot? Like Chris?"

"I think," Rick said, "that Wilson isn't tagging anyone right now with that dubious honor. Actually, I think it's more a case of no one's going to get lonely at the top of that suspect list. Between the council members, Nancy's family, and anyone else associated with the OEI deal, Wilson seems to have his pick of villains."

Who would have thought? With every day that went by, it seemed like the circumstances and people surrounding Nancy Olson's murder got messier and dirtier. Right here in little Savage: big stakes interest groups, bribery, murder. If I threw in what Chris had told me about Stodegard, I could even add blackmail, not to mention very expensive suits. At least some of the heat on Chris was now being shared with his father, I thought, following Rick and Alan to the showers.

But where did that leave Dani?

Answer: At home with her father—the man who now commanded a big piece of Detective Wilson's attention.

A man who might have killed her mother.

And gotten paid to do it?

My stomach turned, and I leaned against the wall of lockers for a moment. Family dysfunction was one thing, but murder for money?

Dani, I decided, needed to be out of the whole mess, and she needed it now. Question was: What could I do about it?

Answer: Nothing.

Zero.

Zip.

Nada.

I hate feeling helpless, and I was feeling it now, big-time. When students tell me they feel helpless, I tell them it's only a feeling and not a fact, that there are always options if you can just find them. I took a few deep breaths, trying to clear out my head, as well as the nausea. I needed to look for the options.

The goal was simple: keep Dani safe. If her dad was homicidal, for whatever reason, she wasn't safe with him. I was confident Chris wouldn't hurt her, but until the murder was solved, he probably wasn't a good choice for refuge for Dani. Besides, if I had become the murderer's target just because I'd spent time at her brother's trailer, the last thing I wanted to do was risk putting Dani in a similar position. I also knew from previous conversations that she had no other family in town, and I wasn't about to suggest she try to move in with family elsewhere. Dani needed all the comfort and support she could get right now from familiar surroundings and daily routine.

That left her friends.

Mandy the mindless and Alicia the tissue queen.

I stifled a groan.

Oh, well. Any port in a storm, at this point. Dani sure as hell couldn't come stay with me. Not only would I have a professional ethics board breathing down my neck for the rest of my natural life, but Chris just might decide I needed a few more punches for good measure.

No, the way to go here was to ship her off to Mandy or Alicia for a few nights.

If nothing else, I'd know that Dani wasn't sitting alone at night in her dad's house waiting for him to show up from the casino. I knew I'd feel a lot better, and I was pretty sure Dani would, too. I resolved to call the girls down to my office later in the morning and talk to them about it.

At the same time, I knew it was just a stop-gap measure. The only thing that would really help Dani was finding out who killed her mother. I knew the police were working on it, but without a witness or a weapon, their investigation could only progress so far.

In the meantime, Dani's life was in limbo, and mine would be in jeopardy every time I talked with Chris.

Except this was nothing like a game show. I couldn't just point to the big board and say, "Killers for two hundred," and have the name of Nancy's murderer pop up.

Instead it occurred to me that, in some ways, finding Nancy's killer was turning out to be like chasing warblers in spring migration. At first, you see all the obvious birds, the Redstarts, the Yellow-Rumped, the Black-and-White Warblers. Their markings are so clear, you can't mistake them for anything else. I guess that's where a murder investigation starts—seeing the obvious suspects. In Nancy's case, that was Chris and Pete Olson, her son and husband.

Then, you start looking for the less visible warblers, because you know there are always more hiding in the trees. You catch a look at one, note the visual clues, and then, if you're still not sure, you listen for the song. That's like what Wilson was doing now—looking between the leaves for more suspects, listening to the tips he was turning up, doing more checking on everyone involved with the OEI deal. Whether or not he'd be able to identify a killer from those cues and clues, though, was a tough call. Especially when some suspects—just like some warblers—could fool you into thinking they were somebody else just from the sounds they made.

When you misidentify a bird, though, nobody's life is hanging in the balance. Birds don't shoot at you when you guess wrong about who they are. They don't punch you in the jaw. Correctly identifying birds is a no-body-contact hobby. It's a passion. Entertainment.

Identifying killers is deadly serious. Literally.

That's why highly trained professionals, like Detective Wilson, did the job, and not high school counselors like me. Unfortunately, this particular high school counselor kept finding himself in possession of information that might be pertinent to the detective's murder investigation. I'd passed along Bridget's comments, and now I had to figure out what to do with Chris's story about Stodegard. I knew Wilson was aware of the exchange between Nancy and the realtor at Dandorff's farm, but without hearing Chris's story of Stodegard's attempt to bribe him, would the realtor slide beneath Wilson's radar and slither away? Whether or not he was involved in Nancy's murder, the scum still deserved some police scrutiny, I thought.

Scrutiny?

Nah.

Arrest?

Now you're talking.

"Time's a-wasting, White-man. You better hit those showers before first bell rings."

Startled, I realized that Alan was standing in front of me, vigorously rubbing his wet head with his towel. "Time flies," he said.

"When you're having fun," I finished for him.

Time was flying this week, all right, but it wasn't fun. Nancy's murder had definitely set other things in motion, and after my experience yesterday afternoon at the trailhead, Wilson had to be pushing hard, collecting information, trying to find some concrete evidence to make an arrest. The only question left was who he was going to settle on as his prime suspect. Chris? Pete?

Stodegard?

As I walked into the shower, another thought hit me. Was I committing a crime by not telling the police what Chris had told me? It wasn't like I was withholding evidence, because I had no proof of anything he'd claimed. At the same time, it might give Wilson something he could use in his investigation. I shook my head, remembering a promise I'd made to myself in the aftermath of the Duluth case: tell the police everything you know. Everything. But right now, I wasn't exactly sure what I did know, only what I suspected. Could withholding my suspicions warrant my arrest?

Actually, I did know one thing for sure: if I got arrested, Mr. Lenzen would have my head—not to mention my job—in a nanosecond.

I blew a very heavy sigh through my lips.

Making it to my office before the first bell was the least of my worries.

CHAPTER EIGHTEEN

Now, this was the life.

The sun was shining, and the warm air flowed gently around me, barely stirring the spring grasses and the new leaves in the trees. A cluster of American Goldfinches chirped in the bushes off to my right, and to my left an Ovenbird was calling *teacher, teacher, teacher.* I was chasing a Cerulean Warbler, and for sixty minutes, I could forget about murder, mayhem, and job security.

Luce had called me at work mid-morning to tell me she'd seen a posting on the list serve for the Cerulean. Finding one this early in May would be unusual, since they're uncommon to rare anytime, but when they are seen, it's usually later in the month. I'd promised Luce I'd meet her at noon at Hanrehan, where the warbler had been found, if she'd bring me a bag lunch. She had—a heavenly sandwich of honey ham, smoked turkey, and apple slaw—and I did, and here we were, warbling over my lunch hour.

"It's awfully accommodating of this bird to be hanging out so close to the high school," I told Luce. "I can't remember the last time I ducked out for a quick bird chase during my lunch hour."

"Location, location, location," Luce replied. "I guess birds are just realtors at heart. Or is it the other way around?"

Hearing the word "realtor" brought Stodegard to mind and the fact that Luce had lunched with him last week.

"So, what's up with Stodegard, Luce? Is he just your everyday realtor looking to close the big sale that'll make him rich beyond his wildest dreams? Or does he have something else going on with OEI?"

Luce studied the trees beyond the trail, then lifted her binos. She was completely still for a moment, then dropped the binos back to her chest.

"What do you mean?"

"Oh, like, is he thinking he might be moving to Chicago and a corporate spot with OEI if this deal goes through? You know, unbridled ambition and the unscrupulous morals to match?"

She gave me a sidelong glance. "Is this about Lily? I know you don't think much of Eric to begin with, but 'unbridled ambition and the unscrupulous morals to match' is a bit strong, don't you think?"

I looked up in the trees and considered for a minute. "No."

Luce laughed. "Eric is the realtor for OEI's acquisition of the property, Bobby. As such, yes, he stands to make a hefty commission. As for the other stuff he's doing for OEI—like checking out Maple Leaf and getting landscaping bids—I'm not sure in exactly what capacity he's doing that. He says he's the point man for the company."

She studied the trees again, lifted her binos, then dropped them once more. "My guess is that he's hoping that, if he can deliver the property along with a full development package, OEI might hire him to be the on-site manager of the whole project."

That would be quite a leap up the corporate ladder, especially for someone who wasn't already a part of the company's management team. Chances to make those kinds of career moves weren't exactly plentiful around Savage. So Stodegard was definitely playing for high stakes. But how much was he willing to gamble? According to Chris, bribery and blackmail weren't out of the question, but could the realtor ante up to murder?

"What do you think about Stodegard, Luce?"

"As a businessman?"

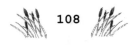

I gazed up at the branches reaching high across the trail. I thought I heard a faint call that sounded like the Cerulean Warbler. "Ssh. Listen."

A moment later, the call was clean and pure. There was no mistaking the short, fast, accelerating series of buzzy notes which ended with a single, long *buzzzz*.

I turned to Luce with a big smile on my face. "We got it. It's definitely the Cerulean. Maybe it'll come closer. Let's just wait a couple more minutes."

And since I had the time, and the bird, and the woman, I gave Luce a kiss while we waited. Like I said, this was the life.

"About Eric . . ."

"Who?"

It took me a second to remember what I'd been asking her, and not just because she used the guy's first name. Looking at Luce in the spring sunshine, it was easy to forget about county politics and big real estate deals. Looking at Luce, I could only think about how natural and good and totally satisfying it felt to have her in my life. That I wanted her in my life forever.

I wanted to marry Luce.

"Eric Stodegard. You asked me what I think about him."

"Oh, right." I shifted my mental gears away from the contemplation of marriage and back to murder.

"Right," I repeated, trying to remember what I had been asking her, and why. "I wanted to know if you thought Stodegard is the type of man who would do whatever it took to get what he wanted."

"Are we talking about the OEI deal or Lily?"

I hesitated, silently reminding myself that Luce, as Lily's friend, was probably privy to a lot more personal information about my sister than I might really want to know.

"Let's start with OEI," I said, opting for the less dangerous route first. "You said that last week, Stodegard told you the OEI proposal was a done deal. Last night, I was at the county council meeting, and frankly, I didn't see it that way at all. Only one out of the four council members was vocal about supporting the project, but Stodegard didn't seem rattled about the upcoming vote at all, just about getting it done as soon as possible."

Luce cocked her head, listening to the Cerulean's call. "He's getting closer."

I listened, too. The warbler's song was louder now.

"When we had lunch with him, Eric told me and Mitch that he had two votes in his column for sure," Luce explained, "leaving two against him and one undecided. Arne and Nancy were the two against, he said. To pass the proposal, then, he needed the undecided councilperson, and he seemed confident that was going to happen. That's all I know. He didn't say who were his sure votes and who was undecided."

We waited another minute, but the Cerulean didn't show himself, and my lunch hour was slipping away. I took Luce's hand, and we started walking back to the cars.

So Luce's impression of Stodegard's confidence matched mine. For all I disliked the realtor and his big client's intentions, he hadn't seemed like a desperate man at the meeting last night. And the only way that made sense was if he already knew that the final vote from the council members would seal the deal in his favor. Last night, his concern had been to expedite the vote. There'd been a noticeable lack of the hard sales pitch I had been expecting. That, I surmised, meant he knew he didn't need to make the pitch, that the votes were already in his pocket. He'd told the council members instead that OEI was anxious to close the deal, but perhaps he was the one who wanted closure more.

And why wouldn't he? From all accounts, he was expecting a very big payday.

And yet, I wondered. Was there a chance the deal wasn't as sealed as Stodegard had assumed? Was he worried that his votes might slip away if there were any delay in the council making its decision? I couldn't believe that he was genuinely threatened by Karl's survey. Despite my own bias and hopes, I was pretty sure that Karl's appeal was too little, too late. Typically, in county deals of this magnitude, eleventh-hour bids couldn't overcome the weeks of campaigning and maneuvering that had gone before.

And if what Luce said was true, that Stodegard was already assuming he had the third vote last week, then Nancy's vote wouldn't have factored in to his confidence level at all. With the three votes he already needed to carry the proposal, there would have been no reason for him to go to Chris last Friday to try to force Nancy's support.

But Stodegard hadn't gone to Chris, I reminded myself.

I mean, he had, but only because Chris asked him to come. Stodegard didn't initiate the contact last Friday night.

Because he no longer needed Nancy's vote.

Pieces of my conversation with Chris popped into my head. He'd said that Stodegard had told him he didn't need him anymore. And that would certainly be the case if the realtor already had his third vote, which would confirm what he'd said to Luce earlier in the week, that the proposal was a "done deal."

As for the part where Stodegard told Chris to forget they'd ever met, maybe that was the real reason he'd come to the trailer on Friday: to let Chris know that any attempt to blackmail him— Stodegard—for his attempted blackmail of Nancy, wouldn't work. If Chris said anything to anyone, Stodegard would deny it, which would only damage Chris's credibility even more. With Chris planning to go to court to get custody of Dani, the last thing he needed was a high-powered local businessman calling him a liar.

Which all meant that the bottom line for Stodegard was that he had no reason to kill Nancy Olson. With three votes for his entertainment complex proposal, he didn't need her. Dead or alive.

"You don't like Eric, do you?"

Luce's question put an end to my chain of deduction. I squeezed her hand.

"No," I said. "Actually, I have reason to suspect that his business ethics might be questionable."

That was putting it nicely.

Then again, I'm a nice guy.

And since I'm a nice guy, I figured that sometime, somewhere, I should probably apologize to Eric Stodegard for thinking he had killed Nancy Olson.

But I was still going to find a way to sic Detective Wilson on him for the way he'd treated Chris.

Once a scum, always a scum.

Luce squeezed my hand back. "That and the fact that he's romancing Lily."

I put on my "I'm so surprised!" face. "He is?"

She shook her head. "You are so funny, Bobby. You and Lily act like a couple of wet cats trapped in the same bag when you're together around other people, but I know how loyal you both are to each other. I also know you don't think anyone's good enough for your sister."

"I didn't say that."

"You didn't have to," she assured me. "It's obvious the way you bristle every time she starts dating someone."

I could feel myself bristling.

"So, I'm a little protective. That's all. I don't want her to get hurt by some smooth-talking Don Juan. She's vulnerable, Luce. Don't laugh! She's got her head buried so deep in the sand of running her business, she's blind to ulterior motives. Like Stodegard using a landscaping bid as an excuse to get close to her."

We came out of the woods, and although this trailhead was a different one than the spot where I'd taken the slide yesterday, I put out a hand to stop Luce.

"Just being a little proactive here," I said.

I counted tires. All eight looked fully inflated. There was no one else in the parking area, and no sounds of a car idling anywhere nearby.

"Looking good," I told Luce and walked her to her car. She slipped into the driver's seat of her black Volvo and put the key in the ignition.

"I still don't understand why you think Eric is using Lily, Bobby. Lily's a beautiful, smart, strong woman. Any man would be lucky to have her. And she runs a good business. Eric needs landscaping, and Lily can do the job. The fact that he's attracted to her is no surprise. Don't worry," she told me. "Your sister's a big girl. She can take care of herself."

She closed her door, lowered the window and leaned out to pat me on the chest.

"Besides, Lily's not all that impressed with Eric anymore, if you want to know the truth. She told me last night it was just momentary insanity. Spring fever. Dinner on Monday and coffee on Tuesday morning, and she'd had her fill of him, she said. Apparently because he was so full of himself."

She shifted the Volvo into reverse. "Later, gorgeous."

Well. So Lily had seen through Stodegard after all. I heaved a sigh of relief and mentally crossed out "scare off the scum" on my to-do list.

I hopped into my SUV and followed Luce out to the highway. With a wave goodbye in her rear-view mirror, she roared off towards Chaska and Maple Leaf, while I turned back to Savage. I automatically scanned for patrol cars and hit the gas without thinking before I caught myself and slowed back down. Bad habits die hard, but I was determined to avoid another ticket.

At least for this month.

As I rolled into the parking lot at school, I congratulated myself on my good timing: even with observing the speed limits, I had five minutes before the bell rang to signal the end of the lunch hour. Now that I thought about it, timing really was everything. Timing made things happen. As a birder, my year was dictated by timing. I chased warblers during migration, and I chased owls and arctic ducks in the winter. Getting the Cerulean today had been a sequence of perfect timing—Luce saw the posting shortly after it first appeared, she caught me at work between appointments, we got out to the park within two hours of the sighting, and we found the bird. A bird that normally wasn't there at that time.

That thought stuck in my head.

A bird that normally wasn't there at that time.

Timing was everything.

Especially in murder.

Nancy Olson wasn't normally around the corner from Chris's trailer. From what I had gathered from both Dani and Chris, Nancy avoided any contact with her son if at all possible. Yet whoever killed Nancy knew where to find her last Friday night, on her way back from seeing Chris. The police had ruled out a random attack from the very beginning of the investigation because Nancy's possessions were undisturbed in her car, and her body had been removed from the scene. If it had been a random killing, the police reasoned, the killer wouldn't have bothered to try to hide the corpse.

As it was, the fact that her body had been deliberately dropped in a place not frequently visited seemed to indicate that the killer wanted her murder to remain undiscovered. If Nancy's body hadn't been found, the police would have had to treat her disappearance as just that—a disappearance—and not a murder. Disappearances were handled differently than murders, Rick had told me once. When it involved an adult, more time was allowed to pass before a full investigation could be launched; it wasn't a crime for someone to be missing. The real problem for the police, then, was that in those cases, by the time the detectives got involved, too many clues were usually lost, and evidence would have vanished, making it nearly impossible to solve the crime. Fortunately for the police in this case, Nancy's body had turned up very shortly after her death, proving they wouldn't have a disappearance on their hands, but a murder.

Unfortunately for us, my mother was the one who found it.

So who had the perfect timing to find and shoot Nancy Olson around the corner from Chris's trailer? Who knew Nancy would be there?

Chris.

Pete.

Maybe Stodegard, if he'd passed Nancy going to see Chris, as he was leaving.

I'd now deduced that Stodegard had no motive, however, and I believed Chris was innocent, leaving me again with Pete Olson.

Then I remembered that Dani hadn't shown up for her standing appointment with me this morning. Was she in school and simply forgot, or was she at home with her dad? I'd talked with Mandy, and she said Dani could stay with her for a couple days, no problem. I wanted to let Dani know.

Especially since I now wanted to talk to her dad.

Alone.

About Friday night.

And why he sent the police straight to his son when they told him his wife had been murdered.

CHAPTER NINETEEN

By the end of the school day, Dani still hadn't shown up in my office. I checked the attendance record and found that she hadn't been in any of her classes, but no one had called her in sick, either. Calling her home phone only produced an answering machine, so I called her cell. All I got there was her voice mail. Finally, I called Chris, but he had no idea where she was, nor had he seen her since Tuesday morning.

He didn't exactly relieve my growing anxiety.

It was true that I felt uneasy about Dani being alone with her dad, but I honestly didn't think she might be in danger from him. Now I found myself wondering if she knew differently. When I'd last spoken with her on Monday night, she had insisted on her father's innocence, yet I'd felt a definite undercurrent of tension from her, like she'd been looking for reassurance from me. In retrospect, I wondered specifically what reassurance Dani had been looking for—reassurance that I believed what she said?

Or reassurance that her dad hadn't killed her mom?

Or was it even simpler—reassurance that no matter what else was going on, she could count on me in her corner?

I'm doing my best, Dani, I thought.

Another piece of my conversation with Chris came back to me. He'd said Dani was always trying to make things look nice, that she was really good at making things look better than they were.

No surprises there. Dani had a dysfunctional family. A standard coping skill kids in those situations developed was the ability to paint their stark reality in more acceptable, although frequently imaginary, hues. Kids like Dani were pros in glossing over ugly details, manufacturing justifications and/or excuses for what they endured, or learning to hide it all behind an appearance of normalcy. The only way I'd been tipped off to Dani's real situation was Alan's request for intervention when her grades dropped; if it hadn't been for that, I'd never have realized how needy she was. The fact that she'd spilled her guts to me so quickly in our developing a counseling relationship was an undeniable acknowledgement of how isolated she'd been, trying to keep up the false front of the family. And when her mom kicked Chris out, it was the last blow for Dani, the one she just couldn't dodge or manage on her own.

Her school work took a direct hit.

Thankfully, she hadn't been beyond help. Between her sessions with Ms. Theis and me, Dani had gotten a good dose of emotional and psychological support, enabling her to get back on track with her studies. Even more impressive, I thought, was the way Dani had now been holding up since her mother's murder. She'd been amazingly assertive with me, willing to ask for the help she and Chris needed, and independent enough to start making some of her own tough decisions, like staying in her own home instead of bailing on her dad.

Which, right now, I wasn't feeling too crazy about.

And which, right now, given her unknown whereabouts, was making me feel very worried.

Had Dani run away?

I didn't think so, but even if she had, I had to believe she'd run to Chris. Chris would do anything to protect her, and Dani knew it.

I knew it, too. I had the bruise to prove it.

What I didn't have at the moment, though, was any more time to speculate about what was going on with Dani today. The Lady Bass had a game across town against our archrivals at Drake, and I needed to have my head in the ballgame by the time we got there.

Not that my brain was going to get us a win, but it might be able to come up with a decent defense once I saw what Drake had for us. I'd never admit it to anyone, but my goal at this point in the season was to keep our opponents from scoring in the double digits. I'd long since learned that "offense" and "Lady Bass" were mutually exclusive terms.

I left a voicemail for Rick about my concern for Dani, figuring he was in a better position to track her down anyway. When the last bell of the school day rang minutes later, I grabbed my duffel bag to head to the locker room to change. I passed Alan's room and saw him sitting on a desk by the door, staring into space, smiling. I stepped inside and waved my hand in front of his face.

"Earth to Alan."

His eyes focused on me. "Yo, White-man."

"I've got a game at Drake, so I've got to run. You okay?"

He sighed and shrugged. Rubbed his hand over his eyes. "I don't know if I'd call it 'okay.' More like shell-shocked. But in a good way. Really. Really a good way. Actually, a great way. I'm just not sure where I'm going to go with this. Or where it's going to take me. But I sure know I want to go."

I blinked.

"Correct me if I'm wrong, but you're not speaking English here, are you, Alan? Because I don't have a clue what you're trying to say."

To my surprise, he burst out laughing. "Oh, man, are you going to love this one."

I was right this morning. Something was definitely going on with him.

Something weird.

"I've got to go, Hawk. But I will call you later," I promised him.

"Sounds good," he said, but I could tell he had already tuned me out. He was back to staring into space, a big smile spreading across his face.

"Really weird," I told myself, hustling out of his classroom and through the halls to the locker room.

Thirty minutes later, I was riding the team bus on our way to Drake, a private high school in one of the northern suburbs of Minneapolis. Behind me, a gaggle of girls were laughing and shouting across the bus aisles, comparing notes on guys, nail salons, dress styles, and limousine companies. Prom was only two weeks away, and the female teen hormones were reaching critical mass.

Too bad I couldn't bottle it. All that energy zinging around on the bus would have been awesome channeled into my players' swings and throws. With that kind of intensity and focus, we'd be formidable on the field. With that kind of adrenaline fueling their play, the Lady Bass could really bite some sssshhh.

Wishful thinking, I knew. It was more than obvious from the conversations around me that softball took a seat way in the back of the bus when it came to planning which hotel was going to be the site of the after-prom shindig. Instead of moving all that anticipatory energy onto the field, it was going straight to my ballplayers'—ah—fluttering insides.

And at this rate, I half expected them to sprout wings en masse and fly out the bus windows.

"I need a tan," the player sitting behind me yelled to her teammates.

"There's a pre-prom tanning special at Hot Bods," someone yelled back. "Show them your prom ticket, and you get twenty-five percent off five sessions."

I heard a shuffle in the aisle, and Bridget landed in the seat behind me while the Player to Be Tanned Later went to get the scoop on the Hot Bods deal.

"Hi, Coach."

"Bridget. Ready to show off that new and improved swing we've been working on?"

"You bet. Especially since my Grandpa's going to be there."

"And Karl!" called out two girls across the aisle.

Bridget's cheeks went bright red.

"Karl just asked Bridget to prom, Coach!"

I nodded and smiled at Bridget. That's my standard response when I get caught in the middle of these kinds of girl conversations: I nod and smile. What else can I do? Ask where she's getting her hair done? Comment on how hot the guy is?

I don't think so.

"He's really nice, Coach. He's so smart, too."

Yup. She definitely had that "stars in her eyes" thing going on.

"I know, Bridget," I told her. "He's a great guy. I'm sure you'll have a wonderful time at prom with him."

"Wasn't he amazing at the meeting last night?" She was warming up to her topic now, a big dreamy smile spreading across her face. "He was so—I don't know—grown-up or something. I can just imagine him being a senator some day, can't you? He wants to be the president of the United States. Did you know that?"

Just for a second, she reminded me of Alan. Not her face, but her smile. Alan had had the same dreamy look on his face when I left him in his classroom before I got on the bus.

No.

Yes!

Please, say it ain't so.

Alan had spring fever.

I stifled a groan. It was bad enough having to deal with teenagers whose brains went to mush, but having to put up with Alan in a crush was downright painful.

I had a vivid memory of nursing him through spring fever our senior year in college. For three weeks, I was afraid he'd either flunk out, get arrested for stalking the poor girl, or kill himself while trying to climb into a sixth-floor dorm window to prove his devotion. Fortunately, none of those things happened.

What did happen was when he finally did get a date with the girl, halfway through the evening, Alan realized she was no rocket scientist. Great hips maybe, but the attic was empty. Close on the heels of that realization came another: he wasn't interested in empty attics. Ever since, he'd made a point of only dating women with at least a master's degree, though if they were short a few credits, he'd give them the benefit of the doubt if the hips looked good. And, as far as I knew, he had never succumbed to spring fever again.

Until now.

Like I didn't already have enough on my hands with Dani being MIA and her mother's killer still at large. Not to mention having to watch my back every time I walked out of Murphy-Hanrehan after chasing a warbler. Now my best friend was going to need a keeper. Didn't Alan know this was not a good time for me? Couldn't he have the consideration to keep his life uncomplicated until I got mine straightened out?

Some friend he was turning out to be.

I mean, geez, he wouldn't even let me borrow his new car.

I bet Mandy would.

Before I could get too steamed up, though, the team bus pulled into the lot at Drake, and we unloaded the Lady Bass and our equipment. After forty minutes of warm-ups, we settled into the dugout and the game got underway. By the bottom of the fourth inning, neither team had scored any runs, but my outfield had actually stopped a few balls, one of which got rocketed back in to make a double play to get us out of the inning.

The girls were ecstatic.

I was stunned.

As the new star in my outfield came into the dugout, I clapped her on the shoulder. "Where did that arm come from?" I asked her.

"She's been lifting weights, Coach," my catcher informed me. "Her prom dress is strapless, and she wants her arms to look buff."

Now, why didn't I think of that? If I'd known strapless dresses were the key to a winning outfield, I would have taken the girls shopping myself.

Months ago.

Last fall.

Last spring, even.

Forget running the practice drills.

Buy them strapless dresses.

Anyway, the girls were so excited after that, I was afraid they'd forgotten we still had three innings to go, let alone needed some runs, before we could put the game in the win column.

I didn't have long to worry, though. Our first two batters got solid hits to take their bases, and then, thanks to an increasingly flustered Drake pitcher, our third batter walked to first base. For the first time all season, we had bases loaded and no outs.

The Savage crowd went wild.

CHAPTER TWENTY

Our screaming fans were on their feet. "We're the big bad Bass, gonna bite you in the ssshh!"

Bridget grabbed her bat and walked up to the plate.

I took a quick glance up into the stands and saw Dandorff and Ray in the bleachers, cheering the team. Next to them was Janssen, who was also shouting encouragement to the girls. Apparently, he'd just come from work—his pressed suit jacket looked a little out of place next to Dandorff's and Ray's knit sport shirts. Especially when he had topped the jacket with his Go Bass hat. The rubber fish flopped on his head as he turned side-to-side to exchange excited remarks with fellow Bass boosters. Two rows below them, I spotted Karl with a bunch of his buddies.

Next to home plate, Bridget dug in and watched two balls go by.

"Good eye! Good eye, Bridget!" Dandorff was calling.

A third ball came sailing at her. She swung.

Missed.

The crowd moaned.

Bridget reset her stance. Another pitch, this one right over the plate. Bridget swung.

The ball shot out between second and third, bounced, got picked up and thrown in.

It was just wide of the catcher.

A Lady Bass dived for the score, and Savage had its first run of the season.

Mayhem.

The girls were screaming and hugging each other. The fans were screaming and hugging each other. Out on first, Bridget was pumping her fist in the air. I caught her eye and held up my arms for her to see and gave her the two thumbs-up sign.

"Batter up!" the umpire yelled over the din of the happy Bass.

Totally focused on the game itself now for the first time in the season, the Lady Bass managed to bring in two more runs in the inning. Hanging tough, we weathered the rest of the game to post our first win: Savage 3, Drake 2.

There would certainly be joy in Savage tonight.

Even as the two teams lined up to shake hands, our exuberant Bass fans poured onto the field. I caught a few backslaps myself as I made my way back to the dugout to collect our gear. Out of the corner of my eye, I could see the tail of Janssen's rubber bass bobbing up and down above the heads of the girls as fans and players alike celebrated our surprise victory over our archrivals.

While the rest of the girls were still milling around the infield, hugging and getting hugged, I sat down on the dugout bench next to Alicia—Dani's friend—who also happened to be our team statistician.

"Cool, huh?" I asked her.

She looked up with a grin. "Yeah. I finally get to put some numbers in the run column."

"Say, Alicia, do you know where Dani was today?" I asked. More often than not, it seemed, students knew each other's whereabouts a lot better than teachers and parents did. "She missed her appointment with me, and it's not like her to miss without letting me know."

She considered for a moment, then shook her head. "Don't know. I guess I didn't see her today, either."

A ripple of unease curled through my belly.

"You know, Coach, we should get Dani on the team. She would be great in the outfield." She gathered up her notebooks and pens and dumped them in her duffel. "When I took gun safety classes with her last fall, she hit the target every time we had shooting practice. And she's strong, too. I bet she could field out in right and throw it in to the pitcher every time. Her aim is dead-on."

The ripple in my belly turned to lead.

"Gun classes? Dani knows how to shoot a gun?"

"Oh, yeah. She's really good, too. Her dad's been taking her hunting with him since she was eight. Last Friday afternoon, before her brother picked her up at Mandy's, she was telling us about the new gun her mom just got. She said it was a sweet little pistol, and she couldn't wait to try it out."

My stomach hit free-fall and I leaned forward. I took one deep breath after another until the wave of nausea passed.

"Coach? Are you all right?"

The alarm in Alicia's voice helped me regain some sense of place while the spinning sensation in my head and stomach slowly receded.

Dani knew how to shoot a gun. So did her dad. So did Chris. So did her mother. And there were guns in her home.

Great.

Guns and a dysfunctional family.

A disaster waiting to happen.

Not any more.

It already had.

I looked at the previously-untapped virtual fountain of information formerly known as Alicia sitting next to me.

"Alicia."

"Yeah?"

Where did I start? Dani and guns? Dani and Chris last Friday? Nancy's new pistol? Dani in the outfield?

"Alicia," I said again, straightening up and turning to face her. "I need you to tell me whatever you can about last Friday afternoon." Another thought struck me. "Have you, by any chance, talked to the police about anything about Dani?"

"No. Why would I do that?"

"Just wondering, that's all."

Then, just when my stomach finally righted itself, I felt it dip again. I'd stumbled, albeit completely unwittingly, on a stone unturned in the police's investigation into Nancy Olson's death. A stone named Alicia. Detective Wilson should be hearing this, I thought. He would, I promised myself, if Alicia had any information at all that might shed some new light on the case.

"Friday, Alicia. What happened Friday?"

"Well, it started in second hour when Ms. Pelling told Mandy to go to see you because her top was cut too low and everyone could see her—"

"No," I interrupted her. "I mean after school, Alicia. What happened after school?"

According to Alicia, she and Dani had gone to Mandy's after school to watch television and hang out. Dani had told the girls about the new gun her mom had and how her mom kept the gun under the driver's seat in her car – "just in case," her mother had told Dani. She warned Dani not to mention the gun to anyone, so Dani figured that meant her dad didn't know about it, and she speculated to the girls that maybe her mom was finally afraid she was pushing her dad too hard about the gambling at the casino and wanted protection—either that, or she planned to use it to threaten him into quitting the gambling.

"Did Dani think her dad might hurt her mom?" I asked when Alicia stopped to take a breath.

"I don't think so. Not really. She said their fights were getting louder, but she'd put money on her mom to win a fight against her dad any day."

My heart ached for Dani.

Again.

What kid should grow up laying odds on which parent would win in a fight?

"If you want to know what I think, I'd say the thing that Dani is most afraid of is not being able to live with Chris. He's trying to fix it, you know."

I did know.

"She never wanted her mom to know when she was at Chris's, because it made her mom really angry," Alicia continued. "So on Friday, when Chris picked her up from Mandy's after dinner and took her home to his place for the night, Dani made us promise not to tell her mom if she called looking for her."

Alicia tugged the duffel onto her lap and fiddled with the zipper.

"She called right after Dani left," she said. "We said we didn't know where Dani was."

"You talked with Dani's mom on Friday night?"

She fiddled with the zipper some more. When she finally answered, her voice was a tiny whisper.

"Yes."

"So Dani was at Chris's house Friday night? After her mom called Mandy?"

"Yes," she whispered again. "Dani didn't want us to tell anyone, Coach. Don't tell her I told you. Please?"

"It's okay, Alicia. You did the right thing to tell me."

She stood up with her duffel and walked over to where the rest of the team was still basking in the glory of victory. Dandorff had his arm around Bridget, who was beaming at Karl. Ray and Janssen were standing nearby, with Janssen making a point of shaking the hand of every person who walked past him. A born politician, I thought. Just like Karl. Laughter carried on the air and in the clear spring evening, I could smell lilacs.

Dani was at Chris's place on Friday night.

She'd told me she was at Mandy's, and she'd told the police she'd been with me. If I was supposed to be her white knight helping her and Chris, why hadn't she come clean with me and told me where she'd really been?

Why hadn't Chris?

According to Alicia, Dani had spent the night at her brother's trailer. If that was true, Chris not only had an alibi, he had a witness to substantiate it.

So why hadn't he told the police—or me—that Dani was with him?

After spending time with Chris yesterday afternoon, I could only conclude that it must have had to do with his overriding desire to protect Dani. I couldn't think of anything else that would make him sacrifice a solid alibi in a murder investigation. He must be trying to protect her.

But from what?

Alicia said the thing Dani feared most was losing her chance to live with Chris. If she'd been in the trailer when her mother came to see Chris, she wouldn't have wanted her mom to find her there, which meant she would have hidden.

And if, while hiding, she'd heard her mother threaten Chris with a restraining order, what would she have done? If she'd heard that all her hopes were going to be blown away, would she have resigned herself to helplessness?

If it had happened several months ago, when her mom kicked Chris out, I'd say "yes." From what I had seen when I first started working with her, Dani was unable to do anything about her own needs and wants in her family situation.

Over the last four days, though, my opinion of her coping ability had undergone a startling transformation.

Dani was standing up for herself. She was making decisions.

True, they weren't always the wisest, but she was making them regardless.

And acting on them.

Alicia's comments came thundering back into my head.

Dani hit the target every time. Her aim is dead-on. She couldn't wait to try out her mother's new gun. She was the only one who knew about the gun under the driver's seat.

A gun that had killed her mother? A gun that the police were still looking for?

An awful suspicion began to form itself in my mind.

Was Chris trying to protect Dani from a murder charge?

Shit.

CHAPTER TWENTY-ONE

By the time the team bus deposited us back in the high school parking lot, I'd had plenty of time to simmer and stew, and now I was fast approaching the boiling point. Aside from the obvious—make that enormous—implications and complications of what Alicia had told me and the horrendous suspicion that was now eating away at me, I was angry at both Dani and myself. At Dani, because she hadn't been totally straight with me when I gave her my full trust—now I couldn't be sure how much of what she'd told me was truth, half-truth or outright lie. I'd even gone so far as to put my job in possible jeopardy by defying Mr. Lenzen's directive to keep my nose out of the Olson murder case. Of course, so far I'd been sneaky—I mean discrete—enough not to trip any alarms that Lenzen might catch wind of it, but that didn't diminish the fact that I'd believed Dani was being honest with me.

As if that wasn't already generating enough heat to thoroughly cook my goose—make that well done, as in burned—I was also angry at myself for making two colossal professional blunders: (1) I didn't maintain an objective distance from my student client; and (2) I'd conveniently and carelessly forgotten what I knew to be classic behavior for a child in a dysfunctional family: the ability to build a fantasy front on an ugly reality.

Or, as Chris had put it, Dani's desire to make things look much nicer than they really were.

Did I know Dani at all?

I had to wonder. The Dani who Alicia had talked about didn't jive with my perception of the Dani I'd been counseling for the last month. To imagine her talking enthusiastically about guns, handling guns or going hunting was scary; the last child I'd want to expose to firearms would be one in a dysfunctional family where anger management seemed to be a pervasive problem. At the same time, it wasn't impossible that Dani was pretending to her friends to be someone else; for an emotionally besieged teen like Dani, the need to be accepted by peers was almost insatiable, and the temptation to do whatever it took to win that acceptance was virtually irresistible.

Which meant I couldn't rely solely on Alicia's information, either. Whether Dani had been honest with her friends was equally questionable.

It occurred to me that the one person I might be able to trust for an accurate assessment of Dani was Chris. He knew how she reacted to circumstances. He'd been her confidante and partner in surviving a rotten home situation. But he was also the one person who, I had no doubt, would lie through his teeth to protect her.

Fortunately, I already knew he was a lousy liar. I made a mental note to call him later.

Meanwhile, it was time to bring in the posse.

I called Rick on my cell phone and asked him to meet me for burgers at Buster's, a dingy little bar that had the best onion rings in town. I made a quick trip to the locker room and changed. When I pulled up to Buster's, Rick's silver Trans-Am was parked next to the door.

"Here's the deal, stud," I said, once we had ordered burgers and rings. We were sitting in a dim booth with red paisley plastic upholstery. "I've got some information about Dani and Chris that I think Detective Wilson should know. Problem is, I need to stay out of it. For reasons of job security. And life security. And tires."

"Stud?" he repeated, choking on an onion ring.

I tugged on my left earlobe.

"Oh. Yeah. Right." Rick touched the small diamond on his ear, then grinned. "I like it. 'Stud.'"

I filled him in on what I had learned from Alicia: Dani being at Chris's trailer Friday night, Nancy calling Mandy's house, Nancy's new gun, and Dani's firearms expertise.

For good measure, I even threw in what Chris had told me about Stodegard—the job offer, his visit on Friday to the trailer, his confident attitude that he no longer needed Chris to pressure Nancy about the OEI deal. To be fair, I also told Rick about Luce's and my conclusion that Stodegard already had locked in the votes he needed for the proposal and, thereby, had no motive to murder Nancy. By the time I was done talking, I had a headache and an appetite for self-pity.

"I'm sorry," I said, "but this detective business sucks. All I wanted to do was be there for Dani, and all I got was deeper and deeper into crap. Now, to top it off, I'm thinking Dani might have shot her own mother. I'm a fool, Rick. I just sucked it all down, everything Dani was feeding me, hook, line and sinker. I don't know what to do. I really have no idea."

Rick finished the last onion ring and washed it down with soda.

"Let me get this straight," he said. "First and foremost, you're afraid that Dani shot her mom."

I nodded.

"Second, you're concerned that you may be criminally liable for not going to Wilson with the information Chris gave you about Stodegard, not to mention the information you now have about Dani."

Again, I nodded.

"Third, and perhaps most troublesome, is the fear that you may, indeed, be a fool."

I started to refute it, but instead, I just nodded one more time.

For a moment, Rick sat in silence, rubbing his fingertips along the edge of the booth table.

"Okay," he said. "Let's take these one at a time. The easiest one first." He looked me straight in the eye. "Yes, Bob, you are a fool."

"Gee, thanks for sharing, Rick. I feel so much better now. I really needed that affirmation."

He was grinning. "You're welcome. I live to serve."

He leaned back in the booth. "As for culpability, you have no concrete evidence or personal knowledge of anything directly related to the actual crime of Nancy's murder itself. What you have is hearsay. Now, that's not to say that what you've learned might not be of value in the investigation, but as far as incriminating you in any way, you're in the clear."

Some of the tension in my shoulders slid away.

"I think," he added a little guardedly.

"As for Stodegard," Rick continued, "my guess is that Wilson will want to take another look at him. If for no other reason than to put some heat on the guy to behave himself when it comes to setting up business deals. But I have to say, if Chris's story about the blackmail is true, then Stodegard looks like a potential suspect, if you ask me. Who's to say the reason he didn't need Chris anymore was because he'd found another way to accomplish the same objective? You said yourself just now that he had his votes, but maybe he had a back-up plan for insurance in case somebody switched sides at the last moment. It wouldn't be the first time something like that has happened."

He had a point. Despite all Stodegard's posturing, he still hadn't gotten a public nod from either Janssen or Ray about the entertainment complex project. And I had to admit, the realtor didn't seem the type to leave any loose ends hanging. Not for the first time, I wondered what Janssen and Ray really thought of the proposal, which way they were leaning, and why they were still playing their voting cards so close to their vests.

But Rick had one more of my fears yet to address.

"So you don't think my suspicion of Dani has any grounds?"

He looked me straight in the eye.

"There are always grounds, Bob, until the case is solved."

132

I could feel my headache starting to swim.

"But no," he added. "I don't think Dani and/or Chris killed their mom."

My head cleared a little, and I looked at Rick, feeling a small measure of hope for the first time since Alicia had told me about Dani's sharpshooting skills.

"Take it apart, Bob," Rick said. "It doesn't fit together. If Dani shot her mom, it would mean she followed her mom—her mom in a car, remember—from the trailer. Unless Dani took Chris's car, which means Chris would have known about it—not to mention that Dani doesn't drive yet—she would have been on foot. Dani chasing down her mom's car? I don't think so. And if Chris knew that's what she was up to, don't you think he would have restrained her and prevented her from doing something so stupid that would mess up his whole plan of attack to get custody?"

I felt a little more tension easing. I hadn't visualized the whole play-by-play, and to hear Rick spell it out, it made my scenario less convincing.

"Then, if she managed to get her mom to pull over, she'd have to reach under the seat for the gun, if we're assuming that Nancy's pistol was the murder weapon. And Nancy would just sit still for that? Again, I don't think so. Finally, there's no way Dani's strong enough to drag a body that far from the car to the creek. She would have had to go back and get Chris to help her. Possible? Maybe, but not very likely. Sorry, Mr. White, but I don't think it was Dani who did it with the gun on the side of the creek."

I let out a huge sigh and felt limp all over. Rick was right. I didn't believe Dani had done it, either, but I had really needed someone else to agree with me.

"Thanks," I told him. "My gut instinct said Dani was innocent, but I needed a reality check. I put a lot of store in my instincts, you know, but I have been known to slip up now and then."

"You? Say it ain't so."

I scooped up the plastic salt shaker and tossed it at him. He made a neat catch.

"Will you do one thing for me, though? Ask Wilson about the gun. Ask him if they found a pistol under Nancy's car seat. If they did . . ."

I didn't even bother to finish my sentence, because Rick was shaking his head.

"No gun in the car, Bob. No gun anywhere. That's one of the reasons they haven't arrested Chris. They have no murder weapon and no hard evidence to connect him to the crime. Whoever killed Nancy must have taken the gun." He rolled the shaker between his palms. "Which means whoever killed Nancy knew about the gun. Maybe whoever killed Nancy used the gun to do it. That would then mean that the missing pistol is also the gun that fired at you and your tires."

We looked at each other.

"Dani told Alicia she was the only one who knew about the gun," I reminded him.

"Apparently," Rick pointed out, "she was wrong. Think about it. Of course there was at least one other person who knew about the gun."

I shook my head, trying to focus on this newest piece of information.

"Bob, Nancy got the gun somewhere. Someone gave it to her, whether she borrowed it from someone or bought it. That person knew Nancy had the gun."

I tried hard to remember exactly what Alicia had said. I couldn't recall if she had said Dani's mom had bought the gun or just that she got a gun. I added it to my list of questions for the next time I saw Dani.

Which reminded me again that I hadn't seen Dani all day.

"What now?" Rick asked. "You don't look so good. Again."

I told him my concerns about Dani's safety. "I didn't see her all day, Rick. It's not like her to miss an appointment and not get back to me. I'm worried. Nobody saw her. That can't be good."

"I saw her."

134

I could feel my jaw drop. "You did? When?"

"First thing this morning, before first bell. She was going to Gwen Theis's office. I guess she spent most of the day there. I figured this was a good thing. Didn't you get my voice mail?"

Of course I hadn't. I'd been too preoccupied with the Lady Bass's first victory and suspecting Dani of shooting her own mother that I'd totally forgotten to check if Rick had returned my call.

"No," I finally managed to get out, feeling like the fool Rick had already confirmed I was. "I didn't. Great. Dani's okay. I never thought to ask Gwen. Dani's not too crazy about her. I just didn't think . . . I guess I . . ."

"Imagined the worst?" Rick suggested, tossing the shaker back to me.

"Yeah." I caught the shaker and put it back on the table. "I seem to be doing a lot of that lately."

"Buck up, Bob. Things are going to start looking up," he promised. "I'll check for records of gun purchases or permits. If I find nothing, you ask Dani for any details she can give you. I'll tell Wilson I got an anonymous tip about Nancy having a gun and see what he can shake loose. And to top it off," he said, leaning across the table and whispering, "we have a date with a Yellow-breasted Chat."

CHAPTER TWENTY-TWO

It took me only a second to switch gears from murder to birder.

"Say again?"

"Just before you called, I checked my email for the MOU list serve. Arne Bjorkland spotted it at Louisville Swamp. If we go right now, we might get it."

Finding the Chat would be huge for me. Once I had it, the only warbler challenge left on my list for this season's migration would be the Kentucky Warbler.

I was already sliding out of the booth. "I can*not* believe you waited to tell me this."

Rick was ahead of me, making for the door. "Well, you had some pretty pressing stuff to talk about, so I figured I'd wait. You know— I'll show you mine if you show me yours."

"Yours is definitely better, stud."

"You got that right."

Less than twenty minutes later, we parked our cars at the trailhead that led into Louisville. Rick had baited me all the way over, driving nine miles per hour over the posted limit, just taunting me to keep up with him and risk a ticket. Of course, I knew he didn't have a thing to worry about—all the deputies in this part of the county knew his car and wouldn't make a stop; me, on the other hand, they'd love to pull over. I'd kept a lid on it, though, and arrived just minutes after Rick—it sort of reminded me of those math problems everyone jokes

about: if driver A is driving at fifty-five miles an hour and driver B is driving at sixty-five miles an hour, what will be the difference in minutes between their arrival times at point C?

"You know," Rick commented as he locked up his Trans Am, "I was thinking on the way out here that if that OEI complex gets built, all the land around here is probably going to triple in value."

I didn't tell him what I'd been thinking about: driver A, driver B, and the unfairness of preferential treatment for fellow patrol officers. Maybe I should talk to Karl about that. He could make it his next citizen's action group.

"I was also thinking that a lot of these farmers out here are getting on in years, and I expect they might jump at the chance to sell their land for a nice lump sum and retire."

"Probably," I agreed. "I know that's Dandorff's plan."

A plan that would benefit him and his grandchildren but leave the rest of the community a lot poorer in a vanishing natural resource. Every time I thought about what losing that piece of land would mean for future generations, I could feel my resentment towards Dandorff rising. And even though I could sympathize with the old farmer's motivations—and I sure wanted to see Bridget and her siblings go to a good college—it made me angry to think about the end result. For the past few days, I'd been directing most of my anger at Stodegard, but the bottom line belonged to Dandorff: without his property, there was no OEI complex.

Rick and I started walking into the swamp. The air was warm and the sun was still high above the horizon. I could hear Ovenbirds and Tennessee Warblers singing down the trail. It occurred to me that I was birding for the second time today, which almost never happened on a school day—a treat about as rare as finding the Chat.

"What about Kevin Ray? Is it his plan, too?"

I stopped and turned to face Rick. "I don't know. Why?"

"Just wondering." He pointed up the trail. "Arne said the Chat was about two hundred yards past the first burned oak. If Ray sells his land, he'll be in Fat City. I was just thinking about who has the most to gain if the OEI deal goes through. Or the most to lose if it doesn't."

I had wondered the same thing, but only in regards to Stodegard's possible motives to remove Nancy Olson as an obstacle to the deal. I hadn't considered the possibility that Dandorff or Ray might have so much at stake that they would see Nancy as a threat. Trying to imagine either of them making the jump to murder was so ludicrous that I laughed out loud.

"What?" Rick asked.

"I just can't see Bridget's grandpa or his pal in a line-up of murder suspects."

"Stranger things have happened, believe me. After fifteen years on the force, I can almost believe anything of anyone. You learn to keep the possibilities open, Bob."

After scouting around in Louisville for a good forty minutes, it became evident that at least one possibility was definitely eluding us: we couldn't find the Chat. There were plenty of other warblers, all of which I'd already seen this season, but no Chat.

"Looks like a miss," I finally said. "Oh, well. Guess I can't complain too much. With the big win at Drake, I'm batting five hundred for the day. Could be worse."

"I wish I'd been there to see it," Rick said. "The Lady Bass bring one home. That must have been something."

"It was. You should have seen Bridget dig in and swing. I was afraid her grandpa was going to have a heart attack, the way he was yelling and jumping in the stands when she touched first base. And afterwards, the way Janssen was shaking everyone's hand, you'd think the win was all his doing."

"Janssen's always campaigning. He's run for mayor how many times?" Rick stopped walking and put his binos to his eyes.

"What do you see?"

"A Prothonotary Warbler."

"You're joking me. Where?"

"Three o'clock about two-thirds up in that third tree back from the trail."

I lifted my binos. Sure enough, the Prothonotary was there. Large and plump, his markings were simple: golden yellow head and underparts, plain blue-gray wings and white patches on his blue-gray tail. It had been three years since I last found one. I had to believe that scoring one today was nothing but a good sign that I would make my season goal of finding every warbler. I knew the Chat would still give me a run for the money, but I also knew that now when someone had seen it once, it was definitely in range. Next time I'd be out here a lot faster.

We were almost back to the parking area before I remembered what we'd been talking about when Rick caught sight of the warbler.

"What were you saying about Janssen? Oh, yeah. The perennial candidate."

"Maybe it's his hobby, Bob," Rick speculated. "We bird, he campaigns. I'd rather bird—it's a lot easier on the wallet than running for office. I wonder how he manages that. I don't know how much insurance agents make, but I can't imagine it's enough to finance a campaign every four years. Maybe that's why he's cozying up to OEI—if he helps them set up shop, maybe he figures they'll return the favor by giving him some help with the campaign coffers."

"Janssen is cozying up to OEI?"

"Yup." He seemed surprised that I was surprised. "What, you didn't know that? Where have you been? He hosted a Meet-and-Greet for the local Chamber of Commerce to get to know the OEI officers on Monday night."

Monday night. Janssen must have been on his way to the Meet-and-Greet when he stopped by the school fields to check on the team's prep for the game against Drake. He hadn't said anything about a meeting with OEI.

Of course, I didn't ask either.

But he'd mentioned the proposal and what he'd like to do with the increased revenues. Couple that with hosting a meeting for OEI to

meet the local movers and shakers and it sounded to me like I could put Janssen's vote in the pro-project column.

Yet, last night at the council meeting, Janssen had seemed to favor Karl and his concern for preserving the Dandorff property. I guess I had interpreted that to mean he was against the proposal. Then again, Janssen was a practiced politician who wasn't about to alienate anyone, especially a bright young high school student in front of the home-town crowd; playing both sides of the fence was probably his stock-in-trade when it came to local hot potatoes. But now, if I tagged Janssen as a sure vote in OEI's (and Stodegard's) pocket along with Ray, who I had figured was supporting the proposal for his friend's sake, then it finally made sense that Stodegard had told Lily and Luce it was a done deal last week. It would also explain why he didn't need Chris any more, either.

Not because Stodegard had some goon waiting to knock off Nancy, but because he had all the votes he needed to get the deal done.

Knowing where Janssen stood made all the pieces fit.

Except one.

If Stodegard had the votes, why did he protest when the council delayed making their decision in order to consider Karl's survey? Based on what I knew about Claver, Ray and Janssen's priorities, counting birds wasn't going to make a difference to any of them. And despite Stodegard's warning, surely OEI wasn't about to drop a project of this magnitude just because the approval came a day or two later than expected.

So what was the realtor really afraid of?

Once again, I could only come up with one answer: maybe, just maybe, he didn't have the votes locked up as tightly as he had hoped. Maybe someone he thought he had last week was thinking this week about jumping ship.

Who could it be?

Damn.

I'd forgotten all about Karl's picnic potluck on Mother's Day. If I'd been there, maybe I'd know who the shaky vote was. Karl had said he got a positive commitment from one of the council members there to vote against the complex, and another one was unsure.

True, "unsure" was a long way from commitment, but it wasn't an unequivocal "no," either.

I gave myself a mental head slap for not asking Karl which council member was still considering, since I assumed Arne was the person who had committed. It had to be that member, I now realized, who was Stodegard's potential deal-breaker. And it had to be either Janssen or Ray, the two council members who seemed to be making a point of keeping their voting intention secret.

Not that anyone could blame them. Look what happened to the last council member who publicly bucked OEI.

Nancy Olson wasn't voting for anything anymore.

Then again, nothing had happened to Arne, and he was no friend of the entertainment corporation. If someone was trying to fix a deal, why hadn't they gone after Arne?

Maybe because he wasn't an easy target, or at least, not as easy as Nancy.

At first glance, the automatic assumption would be—and indeed, had been—that Nancy's death was a result of domestic violence, narrowing the suspect list to her husband and son. Everyone from the police to the council members knew the family was dysfunctional, so placing guilt within the Olson household was a logical conclusion. I was as guilty as anyone else in taking that scenario seriously—until I talked with Chris, I had my doubts about him, and not even two hours ago, I was trying to convince myself that Dani herself wasn't a murderer. My own jury was still out in regards to her father, but it just seemed to me that there was too much brewing around the OEI deal to dismiss Nancy's recent stormy history with the entertainment proposal as pure coincidence.

Thankfully, Detective Wilson had agreed with me and taken the information I'd fed him to broaden his investigation. But even so, when it was all said and done, I had yet to achieve the goal I'd promised Dani: to help Chris. And the only way that would happen was to find Nancy Olson's killer. I'd run a hundred scenarios through my head, sifting and shifting faces and connections, trying to line up the motive, means, and opportunity like three cherries in the window of a one-armed bandit. Now, walking out of Louisville, I felt like a player who'd spent the evening in front of the slots without hitting the jackpot once.

And, to make it worse, I was running out of nickels.

Rick must have read my thoughts because he paused with his hand on his car door handle.

"Do you feel lucky?" he asked me.

Lucky was the last word I would have chosen at the moment. "Not really. What do you have in mind?"

"I'm thinking a little visit to Little Six might just hit the spot. What do you say? We could get something to drink, check out the dealers, maybe ask some questions, like—oh—who hangs out with Pete Olson? Besides Kevin Ray, who just happened to know that someone had offered money to Pete to influence Nancy. I just have this feeling that you're missing some key pieces, here, Bob. I mean, hey, if you're betting on a connection between Nancy Olson and OEI, maybe a casino is the place to look for answers."

I could feel the beginnings of a smile tugging at the corners of my mouth, as I realized I wasn't the only one in Dani's corner: Rick was there, right along with me. As a police officer not assigned to the Olson case, however, he had to respect Detective Wilson's jurisdiction and stay out of the investigation.

Either that or be really sneaky about it.

"Deal me in, stud," I told him. "I just might get to feeling lucky tonight, after all."

CHAPTER
TWENTY-THREE

I'd forgotten what it was like to walk into Little Six. I could count on one hand the number of times I'd gone to the casino since I turned legal at eighteen, and each one of those times I'd lost every dollar of the twenty I always brought. I always told myself it was because I was lucky in love—you know, the old saying "unlucky in cards, lucky in love."

Of course, before I met Luce, I wasn't lucky in love, either, but I was always hoping.

Birders are nothing, if not optimists.

Crossing the threshold of Little Six, though, reminded me why I didn't like gaming: it was like stepping into a circus, and I'm the kid who was terrified of clowns.

Brightly colored lights streamed across the casino ceiling and floor, while crowds cluttered the main aisle, which circled through rows upon rows of slot machines, most of which were being intently played by glazed-eyed customers. Around the perimeter of the room, which was about the size of half of a football field, spotlighted raised platforms held the blackjack and poker tables, presided over by gold-vested dealers, most of whom looked to be women in their thirties. Everywhere there was noise: people laughing and talking, the constant whir of the slots, the jingle of tokens, the music playing through the sound system, the occasional blast of an air horn announcing a jackpot winner. Suspended over the heads of everyone, giant-sized poker chips rolled back and forth on a fluorescent track in the shape of the number six.

Like I said, a circus.

"The only thing missing is the clowns," I muttered to Rick, edging my way around a knot of elderly couples who were trying to decide where to begin their evening of gaming.

"Not anymore," he grinned, spreading out his arms. "Here we are!"

I punched him in the shoulder. "Just keep moving."

We made our way to a drink station at the end of a row of slots and bought two glasses of soda. "Where do we start?" I asked, looking out at the waves of people and machines.

Rick, on the other hand, was checking out the nearest card tables. "Let's try that one—the one with the dealer with the short blonde hair."

I looked in the direction he nodded and saw that three of the four chairs at the table were empty. By the time we jostled through the crowd to get there, though, the seats had filled. I turned to walk to the next table and almost knocked over the short white-haired fellow who was right on my heels. He was fairly round, and he started to keel a bit to the side, so I caught his shoulders to steady him. As soon as he regained his balance, he smiled up at me, eyes twinkling, cheeks pink.

"We've got to stop meeting like this," he said in a husky voice.

I laughed out loud. "Eddie Edvarg. What the heck are you doing here? Trying to win another million?"

Eddie laughed too, his big Santa belly shaking under his suit. I noticed that the chest-length white beard he'd been sporting the last time I'd seen him had been replaced by a neat trim that barely shadowed his chin, and instead of his trademark flannel shirt and suspenders, he wore a very conservative and expensive three-piece suit. "Eddie, you've gone uptown on me."

Eddie clapped me on the shoulder. "Naw. Just a temporary aberration, Bob. I'm doing a job here, so I thought I'd look like management. Didn't fool you, though, did it? You got that old eagle eye. Once a DNR man, always a DNR man."

I introduced Eddie to Rick, who'd heard some of my stories about Crazy Eddie Edvarg, although he'd never met him before. An old buddy of mine from years back, when I worked for the Minnesota Department of Natural Resources, Eddie seemed to have a habit of popping up in my life at odd times and places. The last time I'd seen him was just two months ago, when Luce and I had been chasing Boreal Owls north of Duluth. He had a big spread of acres up there where he indulged himself in his hobby, designing cutting-edge surveillance equipment; as one of America's first big lottery winners, Eddie also liked the privacy his place afforded. The only time he left his northern retreat was to take on the occasional project that challenged his unique electronic wizardry skills. Not that he needed the money, of course, but for the simple joy of doing what he loved. More than once, Eddie's pointed out to me that it really is true that money can't buy everything.

Granted, a few million can buy quite a lot.

Take a look at Eddie's personal fleet of Mercedes vehicles, for example.

Or his spread up north.

Or all his high-tech toys.

Or his expensive suit.

I was in jeans and a windbreaker.

High school counselor chic.

You can't buy that with a million bucks.

Though I'd be willing to give it a try.

Finding out that Eddie was currently doing a job at Little Six, however, was, at the moment, better than winning a jackpot to improve my wardrobe. Instead of beating the bushes for dealers or patrons that knew Pete or Ray, I could pick Eddie's brain for names of people at the casino who were acquainted with the two men.

"The police are way ahead of you," Eddie said, after I explained what Rick and I were doing and why. "All our employees have already been interviewed about Pete Olson. Apparently there is still some question about the exact times he was here last Friday night, but the detective was in this morning, viewing our security tapes, trying to track Olson's movements for the night. Seems there's a small window, about an hour in length, that we can't find the man on any of the tapes. The detective wonders if Olson slipped out, hidden in a crowd, then back in the same way. I've been trying to enhance our images, but no matter what I try, I just can't make out a face when the back is to the camera."

"Imagine that," I said. "Something you can't do with electronics."

I clapped him on the shoulder. "But I have confidence in you, Eddie. If anyone can figure out a way to see through the back of some-one's head, it'll be you."

"Actually," Rick said, "it's not the tapes from last Friday night that we're interested in. We were hoping to go back a little further, say within the last month. We wanted to see who Olson talks to here at Little Six. Or more specifically, who talks to him."

"We could do that. Why don't we take our little party up to com-mand central?" Eddie gave me a little punch in the chest. "I've got some gizmos I think you're going to love. Follow me."

Eddie turned away and led us out of the maze of games and peo-ple, up an Employee Only elevator, across a concealed corridor and into his electronic lair, a large circular room that seemed to float above the casino's main floor. Faced with two-way mirrored windows, the room provided a bird's-eye view of the gaming below, and what an observer might miss with his or her own eyes was meticulously record-ed by a series of cameras mounted to the underside of the surveillance aerie, as well as cameras lining the ceiling's perimeter. Inside the con-trol room, banks of monitors displaying real-time images sat beneath the windows; in the center of the room was a console with additional screens, multiple keyboards, a variety of palm-sized devices and lis-tening gear. Eddie went straight to the console and picked up what looked like a remote control.

"Watch this," he said and pointed it through the windows at the blonde dealer we'd left downstairs.

Immediately, the monitor nearest Eddie's outstretched hand displayed the same semi-circle of faces that the dealer was seeing. The resolution was so good, I could practically count the players' eyelashes.

"I'm impressed," I told Eddie. "Remind me to use floss before I come back here. I'd hate for you to see food stuck between my back molars."

Eddie laughed. "If you think the image is good, wait till you hear the sound."

He handed me a tiny headset to put on as he pressed another key on the remote, and I could clearly hear the dealer calling the cards at her table. By some magic, all the other noise I'd heard on the floor below was missing—no background music, conversations or slot machine hum.

I passed the headset to Rick so he could hear it, too. After a moment or two, he let out a low whistle. "Slick," he announced.

Eddie sat at the console, and within seconds, he had a photo of both Olson and Ray on the screen. A few more commands and he had a list of dates and times the men had appeared on the casino's surveillance cameras in the past month. "I think this will go faster if you split it up," Eddie suggested. "Bob, you sit here and view Olson. Rick, I'll set you up on this screen for Ray."

"How did you do that?" I asked. "I can't believe you already had a file on those guys. Well, maybe Olson, if Detective Wilson was here today, but Ray?"

"It's based on image recognition, Bob. That and a software program I designed. I doubt you really want to hear the details."

He was right. Neither computer programming nor electronics have ever been my strong points. In fact, they haven't even been my weak points. When it comes to me and technology, all bets are off.

For the next hour, Rick and I watched our respective collections of Olson and Ray walking into the casino, playing cards, switching tables, making small talk with other patrons and then walking out of the casino. I fast-forwarded everything, pausing only when Olson interacted with another person. My idea was to see if there was any-one he regularly spoke with—if so, then I'd ask Eddie to help me iden-tify the person so I could try to talk with him. So far, though, Ray was the only repeat companion I'd seen. Since my eyes were aching from so much video viewing, I took a break and stretched, then leaned over towards Rick on the stool next to me. "Any luck?"

He shook his head. "The only thing that stands out is how fre-quently Ray comes to Little Six. That, and how much money he must be losing. Where do these guys get the money to burn like this any-way?"

I had no idea. Based on what Dani had told me, her dad didn't have the money, except by taking it from his wife or hocking house-hold items. As for Ray, I didn't have a clue.

Then again, maybe I did.

I remembered that Dandorff had mentioned that Ray had lost his wife. If there had been an insurance payout, it might explain how an old farmer had money to play with. It might also explain his fre-quent visits to the casino; Ray was lonely, according to Dandorff, and it wasn't uncommon to find older singles patronizing Little Six as a venue for socializing, as well as entertainment.

Not my cup of tea, that was for sure. I'd much rather be chasing a bird any day.

"Can you make a guess as to how much Ray has lost?" I asked Rick.

"No idea. Why?"

"I'm just wondering if he's in debt, like he said Olson was. If he is, then he's going to be needing some income to pay it off."

"You're thinking he could sell his land and make a bundle if OEI comes to town."

"Yup."

"And that would be a strong motivator for him to make sure the OEI deal goes through," Eddie offered, completing my theory.

148

"The thought did occur to me," I said. "The question then, is: how strong a motivator?" Could Ray have been in so deep, he would do whatever it took to remove obstacles, including Nancy Olson?

"Bob," Rick cautioned, "Don't you think you might be over-reacting here just a little? Lots of people gamble here, lots of people have debt, but that doesn't mean they're capable of murder. Maybe it's time to call it a day. What do you think?"

I closed my eyes and rubbed my temples. It was almost eleven o'clock. "Yeah, you're right. I'm beginning to feel like I should be asking 'who didn't have a reason to kill Nancy Olson?' instead of who did. Let's just finish these last tapes, and then we're out of here."

I turned back to my screen and felt my eyes blurring as the last of the surveillance tapes sped by. Just before I closed the last entry, a shock of recognition hit me as I looked at Olson speaking with a man dressed in an expensive suit. The way the other man stood, his confident body language, and the suit itself, all rang bells in my head. This man was familiar. I stopped the video.

"Eddie, can you get better definition on this?"

Eddie leaned over my shoulder and tapped a few keys. The photo enlarged and sharpened, but only the very edge of the man's face was caught by the camera as he spoke with Olson. "We've got too much of his back and not nearly enough of his face, Bob. Sorry."

I blew air out of my cheeks and sat back.

"What, Bob?" Rick had turned his screen off and was leaning over to see mine.

I pointed at the screen. "I bet you money that the man talking to Olson is Eric Stodegard."

"And this tape is from when?"

"Sunday night, about midnight." There was something else in the frozen image I wanted him to see even more than the resemblance to Stodegard, however. "Look at their hands, Rick. What do you see?"

He let out a low whistle. "The guy is slipping Olson an envelope. A fat one. Papers? A road map?" Rick gave me a grim look. "A payoff? We know that Olson told Ray on Monday that his money problems were over."

"Did Wilson see this?" I asked Eddie.

"Don't think so. The detective only watched entrance and exit shots to establish alibi times from Friday night."

"He needs to see this. Will you get him back out here?"

"Will do."

I thanked Eddie for all his help and made him promise to join Luce and me for dinner one night next week. As he led us back downstairs, he mentioned that he thought Luce was a keeper and that I'd better marry her before she got away.

"So I've been told," I noted.

"And?" Eddie looked at me expectantly.

"And what?"

"Son, you've got to ask the woman. You know she's going to say 'yes.' What are you waiting for?"

A quiet moment?

A romantic evening?

How about . . . screaming patrons?

Definitely not what I'd had in mind.

CHAPTER
TWENTY-FOUR

The heavy form of a man fell past me, and in the space of a second, all hell broke loose on the Little Six floor.

"Oh, my God!"

"He's shot!

"Blood! Blood!"

"Someone call 911!"

Rick was already in full cop mode, trying to move people away from the man lying face down in a pool of spreading blood. Eddie spoke into his cell phone, giving information to the emergency dispatcher he'd called, and at least five members of the casino's security team were trying to form a cordon around the man on the floor. A moment later, an older fellow in a burgundy sports coat pushed forward towards Rick, shouting that he was a doctor, and Rick let him pass to check for a pulse on the wounded man.

Everywhere, people were swarming. Some pressed forward against the security men to get a better look at the center of the chaos, the man who still lay on his stomach between the gaming tables. Other patrons were rushing towards the exits, hands clutching each other's arms and shoulders. Beyond the immediate area, players at poker tables and slot machines were standing up, necks craning to see what the commotion was all about. Underneath it all, the hum of excitement and fear seemed to feed into the general noise level, making it hard for anyone to clearly hear anything except the screams that still split the air from a group of silver-haired women frozen to the spot about ten feet away from the downed man.

"The ambulance should be here any minute," Eddie shouted to the doctor.

The man looked up from where he had gone on one knee to check for a pulse and shook his head. "It's thready. I don't know if he's going to make it."

"Bob!" Rick yelled. "Get those women off to the side and see if you can quiet them down. Keep them together. We'll need to find out if they saw anything."

I herded the three wailing women away from the bleeding man and the doctor. Finding a vacated table, I helped them each into a chair and told them I was a counselor, that I was going to sit with them until they were calmer. "The police are on the way," I assured them. "I need you to sit tight, take deep breaths and try to remember what just happened."

"A man was killed!" one of the three, a short and plump senior citizen, her eyes wild, huffed at me. "He practically fell into my arms!"

"Please, ma'am," I said to her. "Take some slow deep breaths. I don't want you hyperventilating on me. Breathe with me, okay?" I made a big show of taking in a deep breath and then letting it out.

The other two women joined in, and pretty soon I had them all breathing in unison, the pupils of their eyes not quite as dilated with panic as they had been when we first sat down at the table. I smiled my approval at their efforts.

"Good job," I encouraged them. Breathing lessons for murder witnesses, I thought. If my counseling career was ever totally tanked, I could always teach breathing lessons for murder witnesses.

Not a pleasant thought at all.

Nor was the thought that a man might have been killed not more than an arm's length away from me.

"You were there, too, young man," another one of the ladies said to me. "That man fell towards Edna and you were right behind him. I noticed your lovely auburn hair. Mine used to be just that color when I was your age."

I nodded and smiled.

What else could I do? It worked with my ballplayers.

"Your hair was not that color, Bernie. It was orange. You just wished it was that color." The one who was Edna turned to me and lowered her voice. "She's going senile. Don't listen to her."

"Did you say you were a counselor?" the third lady asked.

"Yes, ma'am. I work at Savage High School."

"I knew you looked familiar!" Bernie cried, clapping her hands together. "You're a birder, too, aren't you? And you've got a bird name. What was it? Lark Bunting? Jim Mallard? Jack Sparrow?"

"That's the pirate, Bernie," Edna corrected her. "You know, the one in the movie with all the black eyeliner."

"It's Bob White," I said. "My name's Bob White."

"That's it!" Bernie clapped her hands again. "I met you on a birding weekend a few years back. There were about four or five cars of us that went up to the northwest tip of Minnesota to find a Northern Hawk Owl." Bernie beamed at her friends. "He doesn't remember me because I was sitting in the front passenger seat of the car, and he and the sweetest young woman were crammed into the back seat with all our birding scopes."

Bernie turned back to me. "I could tell you had eyes for each other. I thought, 'Now there's a match made in birding heaven.' I hope you married that gal."

Unbelievable. Bernie had been one of the group of birders on the weekend I first met Luce. It had to have been three years ago, and almost at the opposite end of the state. What were the chances I would be sitting here with her years later, both of us witnesses to a shooting at Little Six?

Talk about a rarity.

"I'm sure she'd jump at the chance to marry you, young man," Bernie added. "If I were forty years younger, I know I would."

Good to know.

If Luce turned me down, I could always ask Bernie.

"Ladies, Bob." Rick materialized behind me, accompanied by a uniformed policewoman.

"I'd like to ask you a few questions," Rick's colleague said. "Except for you, Mr. White. You can go with Officer Cook here."

"Thanks for the save," I told Rick as we worked our way back to where Eddie was directing his security people. "I owe you again, stud. I think I was going to get a marriage proposal."

Rick didn't respond to my joke with his usual repartee, I noted. Instead, he pulled me aside before we reached the area in the casino that was now sectioned off with yellow crime scene tape.

"You need to know something," he told me, his voice flat. "The man who was shot was Pete Olson. Dani's dad. He's on his way to the hospital, but I don't know if he's going to make it."

Dani's father? Her father was shot? Who'd do that?

I really, really hate casinos.

CHAPTER TWENTY-FIVE

Three cups of coffee later, Rick and I were still back up in Eddie's surveillance aerie, studying all the video we could lay our hands on from tonight, trying to find Pete Olson in the casino and tracking everyone he came in contact with, from the door security personnel to the other gamers at the tables where he played (and lost) at poker to Edna and Bernie brushing past him in the aisles. The most critical piece of footage from the evening—when someone bumped into him and shot him point-blank in the side with a silenced revolver—was, however, obscured by a tall fellow who happened to be standing directly in the line of sight between the assailant and the security monitors.

Me.

"Now, see Bob, this is where your being six-three is a problem," Rick commented. "When we want to identify shooters in a casino, you're too tall for the cameras to see around."

I gave him a sour look. "I'll keep it in mind, stud."

"That does it," Eddie announced. "We get security gates in here starting tomorrow. I've been telling management for weeks we need weapons screening. Those stupid little signs at the entrances forbidding firearms don't do squat if a gunman wants to walk in here and start shooting people. Like tonight."

"I'd say our gunman tonight wasn't looking to start shooting people in general, Eddie," Rick observed. "This was a targeted hit. Quick. Professional. In and out."

155

"Not good," Eddie said.

Not good at all. Whoever Pete Olson had been playing with at the casino wasn't very nice. I looked at Rick, whose thoughts were clearly traveling down the same track as mine. A professional gunman meant the stakes must have been pretty high, and I could only think of one game in town at the moment that might make the cut.

"Now if we can just find out exactly what game Olson had been playing, and with who, we just might be getting somewhere," Rick mused. "I'm calling Wilson. Olson's getting shot might just be the break we need for this case. Assuming he survives, he's got to be ready to spill the beans about what he hasn't been telling us."

"You think he killed Nancy?"

Rick pulled out his cell phone. "If he didn't, I'm betting he knows who did."

The phone in his hand rang.

"Cook here." He listened for a moment or two, concern crossing his face. "Tell them I'm on my way and to stay put. I don't want those kids going anywhere until I see them."

He snapped his phone shut. "I had an officer go out to Chris's trailer to tell him about his dad. Dani's there, too. A squad car is watching the yard. I'm going to swing by the hospital and check on Olson, then head out to the trailer." He stuffed the phone in his pocket. "I don't want those kids to turn up missing tomorrow."

I wasn't sure what he was worried about. "You think they might be involved in their dad's shooting? That they know something about it and would take off?"

"Absolutely not," he replied. "I don't want them to turn up missing tomorrow because they're dead. Look, Bob. In less than a week, their mom has been murdered and a hitman came after their dad. Do you want to take a chance that they're completely safe from harm? Alone in a trailer on the edge of the woods?"

His face was strained with worry. I wondered if Chris and Dani knew how much Rick cared about them.

"Let's go," I said. "I'm right behind you."

CHAPTER TWENTY-SIX

It was after two when I finally hit the bed in my town house. The emergency room doc had told us it would be a while before he had solid news, but at least Pete Olson was still alive. Dani and Chris had offered Rick the couch in the trailer, and he'd opted to stay with them, while I made a beeline for home. For the first time in days, I'd thought I could see daylight at the end of the tunnel of Nancy Olson's murder. After last night's events at Little Six, it'd looked like evidence was mounting to warrant Pete Olson's arrest. When that happened, Chris would be in the clear and could move ahead to make a better life for both himself and his sister. True, there'd be more than enough tough stuff for them both to work through, but at least they could make a start. With that idea in my head, I fell asleep, grateful for Eddie's surveillance talents and hopeful for a better day in the morning.

Less than four hours later, however, I was awake again, listening to the enthusiastic and incredibly loud chorus of birds out in my backyard. Normally, I love to leave my windows open at night for the fresh air, and I like hearing the birds first thing, but this morning, the magic was missing. I pulled my pillow over my head and wished for another three hours of silent darkness.

While I was at it, I also wished that Nancy Olson had never been murdered, that Pete Olson had been a perfect father who didn't gamble, and that Dani and Chris had grown up in a home filled with love and supportive parenting.

157

I wished for peace on earth, too, and gasoline that only cost fifty cents a gallon so I could bird to my heart's delight without breaking my budget, but figured that just might be pushing a little too hard.

As it was, the wish fairy must have been otherwise occupied, because the birds just got louder and my room grew brighter, and I was pretty sure I didn't hear everyone in Savage cheering about the drop in gas prices. I rolled out the side of the bed and raked my hand through my hair as I walked into the bathroom to shave. Midway through my shower, I remembered I was going to call Alan last night and never did—I hoped that my excuse of being caught in the middle of a shooting at the casino would satisfy him. I'd catch him today, though I wasn't sure I really wanted to hear about it, especially if it was a case of spring fever. But Alan was my best friend, so I'd suck it up and listen, no matter how stupid he might get over some woman.

I thought briefly about Luce. I wasn't stupid over Luce. Luce was not a case of spring fever. Luce was the love of my life.

I knew that everyone was right, that I should pin her down and get engaged. I mean, geez Louise, even Bernie, whom I'd run into only twice in my life, said that I ought to be married to Luce. 'A match made in birding heaven,' she'd said.

Well, that may be true, and our mutual interest in birding was probably the first thing that drew me to her, but Luce was so much more than a birding partner to me now.

After three years together, it seemed like she was a piece of every part of my life. And she knew me so well that sometimes, I could swear she even knew what I was thinking before I did.

Okay, I admit that part was kind of scary. The only time I really liked that part was when she knew I was thinking white chocolate raspberry scones would really hit the spot.

And then she baked them up before I had to ask.

So even her knowing what I was thinking was a good thing.

At times.

I remembered what Bridget had said about her grandparents. That all her grandpa had to do was look at his wife and he'd known where he was going.

That was the way I felt about Luce, too. Like Bridget's grandma was for her husband, Luce was my North Star. Even in the middle of a disastrous week like this, all I had to do was think about Luce, and I knew where I was and where I was going.

It was time to marry Luce.

According to Crazy Eddie, all I had to do was ask the woman.

According to Bernie, Luce would jump at the chance to marry me.

So what was I waiting for?

I thought about watching those ducks in Duluth with Luce back in March and her response to my nebulous query about marriage. True, I hadn't exactly spelled it out for her. I hadn't asked her to marry me, specifically. But she hadn't exactly jumped at the general concept, either.

Not then.

Would she now?

There was only one way to find out.

Like Eddie said, all I had to do was ask her.

WHEN ALAN WALKED INTO HIS CLASSROOM that morning, I was waiting for him. He had shadows under his eyes, and it seemed to take him a moment or two longer than normal to focus on me.

To be honest, I probably wasn't in much better shape myself. Even my decision to propose to Luce as soon as possible had only energized me long enough to get me through my shower, shave, and drive to work. "Rough night, Hawk?"

A slow smile lit up his face. "You're here early. Is this the old early bird catching the worm, White-man?"

"Ah, gee, Alan, I wouldn't call you a worm. And even if I did," I paused for effect, "I'm not the one who caught you, am I?"

Alan burst out laughing. "No, you are not. How did you guess?"

"This is me, Alan. Your best friend. How could I not guess?"

I wasn't going to tell him it took me almost a whole day yesterday and Bridget's goofy smile to figure it out. "Please, please, just tell me she's got at least some furniture in the attic. A whole room isn't necessary. A couple of lamps would be nice."

Alan smiled again. "Oh, yeah, she's got furniture upstairs. A whole houseful, I think. Enough to keep me comfortable for a very, very long time."

I sat on the edge of his desk while he stashed his briefcase behind his chair. "Where did you meet her?"

"At the grocery store. Don't laugh," he said when I started to do just that.

"You? Mr. Domestic? I wasn't sure if you even knew what grocery stores were. The closest you come to preparing food is dialing for take-out."

He gave me a dirty look and sat in his chair. "Anyway, as I was going to tell you, before I was so rudely interrupted, I was walking down the aisle . . . okay, I admit it, I was lost in the store. I had no idea where to find the parmesan cheese."

I laughed again.

"Give me a break, here, Bob, it's a new store! Anyway, there I was, and then I saw her, and I thought at first she was just a girl, because she's petite, you know? And she was climbing up on the second to the bottom shelf so she could reach something way up on top, and she started to slip, so of course, being a gentleman, I went to catch her from falling."

I felt an odd sensation ripple down my spine. Some kind of warning.

"Don't tell me she's a student, Alan," I broke in, suddenly alarmed. "That would not be good. That would be very, very bad. I'm still shaking off nightmares about making license plates thanks to Dani."

He gave me an "are you out of your mind?" look, and my relief was so instantaneous, my breath whooshed out, and I almost felt light-headed.

"She's not a student," he said.

"Thank goodness for huge favors."

"Can I go on?"

"Please do. Wait. Let me guess," I said, tapping my bottom lip. "She has great hips. Which you just happened to notice right before you got your hands on them."

For a split-second, I thought Alan was blushing, like a kid caught in the act.

"Well, yeah, if you must know. But I didn't grab her, Bob, I swear. She just sort of fell into my hands. As soon as I caught her, I could tell she wasn't a girl, but a woman. Definitely a woman. And then she turned around and looked at me with these smoky eyes, and I thought, 'Damn! It's her!'"

"Who?"

"My soul-mate. My one true love. You're the one who's always saying I'm a romantic. Well, it's true. I am. I looked in her eyes, and right away, I knew. I'm going to marry this woman. She said to me, 'Thanks for the save, cowboy.' I had my old hat on, you know. I said, 'I'm not a cowboy, I'm a teacher at the high school.'"

"Hey, I bet that impressed the hell out of her."

He ignored my sarcasm. "She looked at me for a minute like I looked familiar to her, too, and I started making small talk—anything to keep her looking at me—and then I walked down another aisle talking with her while she shopped."

Alan leaned back in the chair and laced his fingers behind his head. "And then she went through the express check out lane and out of the store."

"I assume you got her name and phone number."

"Nope. Didn't need it. I knew who she was. So I followed her home, and the rest is history."

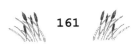

161

"You followed her home from the grocery store?"

"Mr. White?"

I turned to see Dani standing in Alan's classroom doorway. The bags under her eyes were as bad as Alan's and mine. "Dani. I didn't think you'd be in school today. Did you get any sleep?"

"Yeah, I slept some. Officer Cook brought me to school this morning. He thought this might be a good place for me to be today. And he said to tell you that he's got a friend keeping Chris company, too." She brushed a piece of hair off her face. "I forgot to tell you last night. I'm sorry I didn't let you know that I was with Ms. Theis yesterday. I figured you'd know. I promised you I'd talk with her."

I walked to the door and waved her out ahead of me. "I'm glad you did, Dani. I think it'll help a lot." I turned back to Alan and gave him a thumbs up. "Good luck, Hawk."

"I have your blessing, huh?"

"Sure. Why not? It is spring, after all."

Back in my office, I closed the door. "How's your dad doing, Dani?"

She sat in the chair closest to my desk. "He's going to be okay, but he's going to be in the hospital for a while. They said he lost a lot of blood."

I knew. I'd been there.

"Dani, we need to talk."

She pulled on the hem of her T-shirt and glanced around my office. "Okay."

I decided to cut right to the chase. Last night, Rick and I had focused on the two kids' immediate safety. Today I needed information. "Dani, did you see your mom on Friday night?"

Her fingers went still on her hem, and I think she stopped breathing. She wouldn't look at me.

"Who told you that?"

"Nobody. I just want you to tell me. Did you?"

She let out a long sigh and looked at me then. "Yes."

162

"When, Dani?"

"It was at Chris's trailer. After dinner. He picked me up at Mandy's and brought me home with him to spend the night."

She dropped into the chair opposite my desk, while I sat on the front edge of it, facing her.

"My mom hated when I stayed with him, so I always had him pick me up from someone else's place. Anyway, she showed up at the trailer, and I hid in the bedroom because I didn't want her to know I was there. I could hear her and Chris having this really bad fight, and when I heard her leave, I peeked out around the curtains in the bedroom window, and I saw her get in her car and back out the drive." A tear started down her cheek. "That was the last time I saw my mom."

"Were you there all night then?"

"Yes." It was barely a whisper.

"Dani, why didn't you tell the police? You're Chris's alibi. You can prove he didn't kill your mom if you were with him all night. That's what they need to stop suspecting him."

More tears leaked out of the corners of her eyes. "Because he told me not to tell anyone! I'd told my mom about him wanting to take us all to court, and he was angry at me for telling her, so I promised him I wouldn't tell anything he told me not to. When he dropped me off at the house early on Saturday morning, he said not to tell anyone where I'd been. I didn't know my mom was . . . was . . . ." She was crying too hard now to talk.

"Dani, I'm sorry. I know this is all horrible for you, but I need to know what you know so I can get you and Chris all the help you deserve." I felt like a heel pressuring her for information. The kid had lost her mom, her dad was in critical condition after being shot, and I was grilling her.

None of which had even been hinted at in my counseling job description.

"So when the police came," Dani was getting out between sobs, "all I could think was to not tell them where I'd been because Chris

163

told me not to tell. I didn't want to get Mandy in trouble, so I thought about how you'd been helping me, and I thought maybe being with a counselor would be a good answer."

Oh yes, we all knew how well that had worked out. Thankfully, all I had to show for it was a bruise and not a cell-block number. I still owed Rick his beer for that save.

"Then when I found out they thought Chris . . . you know . . . killed Mom . . . how could I tell them the truth? They'd think I was lying for sure." She wiped her face with the tissues I handed her. "And I didn't tell them about the car I saw, either, because I was afraid they'd think I was lying about that too! And now," she took a deep breath, "I'm afraid of my dad!"

"Wait a minute." I put up my hands to make her stop. I'd wanted information, but now there was too much at once.

"What car? Why are you afraid of your dad? He's in the hospital. He hasn't hurt you, has he?"

"No, no. He hasn't done anything to me. But I saw his car follow my mom's away from Chris's trailer." She balled up the tissues in her hand. "He doesn't know I saw it," she added.

Crap. This was definitely falling into the category of "not what I wanted to hear" this morning. Not only had Dani lied to the police and withheld information, but was she also a witness to a murder?

CHAPTER
TWENTY-SEVEN

Dani," I said, "are you sure? Are you absolutely positive it was your dad's car that you saw following your mom?"

Because if it was, I was calling both Rick and Detective Wilson right now to make sure they kept Pete Olson under lock and key. The man might be in intensive care in the hospital, but if Dani had seen his car trailing after her mother's, I wanted to make sure she stayed as far away as possible from him.

"I don't know, Mr. White!" Dani wailed. "I thought it was because it was black and had that same boxy front like my dad's car, but it was getting dark, and I couldn't see for sure. I didn't think about it at all until the police came and told me my mom . . ." She started sobbing uncontrollably.

I leaned forward and gently held her shoulders in my hands. "Dani," I said, "this is going to be over, soon. I promise you. Can you just hold on a little longer and help me out with this? I need you to tell me what happened."

Her sobs subsided. She wiped her face again with more tissues.

"Okay," she sniffled. She took two big breaths and started again. She repeated what she'd said about going with Chris to the trailer, about overhearing the argument between her mother and Chris and then watching her mom's car leave.

"As soon as my mom got out to the main road, I saw another car come up behind her, and it followed her away. It came up behind her

slow, like it had been waiting for her, not like it was trying to pass her or anything. I just assumed it was my dad's car, and I wondered why he was waiting for her, but I didn't think anything more about it. Until the police came," she added. "Then I got scared."

"Dani, did Chris see this other car?" I wanted her to focus on the sequence of events and not jump ahead.

"No. But I told him about it. Later."

"Later when?"

"After the police came to the house." She wiped her eyes once more and balled the tissue up in her hand. "I called him, and he came over, and we talked about it. It was Saturday night, but my dad stayed home, so Chris and I went for a drive, and I told him all about the police and the stuff they asked me and how I didn't tell anyone I'd been at his place the night before. I told him about the car, then, and how I thought it was Dad's and I was scared that Dad might have . . . might have . . ."

She pressed the ball of tissue to her mouth. I watched her fight the tears, push back the pain and fear that must have been eating her alive the last few days. My hands tightened on her shoulders just a little. "Dani, you're doing an awesome job here. I won't let you down. I swear it."

She managed a weak smile. "That's what Chris says, too. I believe you, Mr. White. I believe him, too."

I let her go, and she slumped back in the chair. "Chris made me promise not to tell anyone about the car I saw. He said it would only make it dangerous for me if people knew I saw it."

So Chris had had the same thought I did—that Dani was a witness of some kind. Rather than expose her to scrutiny and possibly even jeopardize her safety, though, he'd been willing to face the police without an alibi and refused to offer potentially incriminating information about his own father. My estimation of Chris's courage and commitment to his sister notched up a few levels higher.

At the same time, knowing how it may have also hamstrung the investigation into his mother's death—not to mention the seriously compromised position it had placed him in—it made me want to smack him. I hoped that if I ever had to go to the mat for my sister (and I would, in a heartbeat, no matter how crazy Lily makes me), I'd have Chris's courage, but a lot more smarts about it.

"Dani, you've got to talk with Detective Wilson about this stuff."

She shook her head. "He won't believe me."

"I think he will," I argued. "We'll get Officer Cook to go with you. He'll back you up. Would that help?"

Dani nodded. Rick had definitely scored trust points with her last night, staying with her and Chris. That was good. Now if she could extend some of that trust to Wilson, he could start getting his leads firsthand, instead of filtered from me through Rick.

Besides, I was really getting tired of being the Source to be Named Later.

What I didn't tell Dani at the moment was that I also wanted her to talk to Wilson about some other things she hadn't discussed with me, but which I knew about thanks to Alicia. In particular, I wanted her to tell him everything she knew about Nancy's new gun.

Like why her mother had it and where it had been hidden in the car.

And gee, if Dani knew where it had come from, that would be a lovely bit of information I'm sure the detective would be happy to hear.

I called Rick's office in the school and got his voice mail, saying he would be out for the day, attending a workshop. I briefly debated calling Wilson directly, but I knew Dani would clam up if he questioned her without Rick there. Despite my assurances, Dani still considered Wilson to be the enemy gunning for Chris. Since I knew that Rick planned to join me for the bird survey out at Dandorff's land in the early evening, I asked Dani if she could meet us there beforehand. She said she'd ask Chris to bring her after she got off work.

"Although it will probably be Officer Cook's friend driving me," Dani added. "He told Chris that they were going to be best friends by the end of the day."

"Thank you, Rick," I said under my breath, relieved to know he had another officer picking up the guardian angel shift throughout the day. "You are covering the bases well, stud."

I opened my office door, and Dani slipped into the stream of students who were in the halls, changing classes.

"Yo, Mr. White!" Karl waved to me over the heads of the students around him. "You're coming tonight, aren't you?"

"You bet, Karl," I called back. "Me and my best birding buddies. Looking forward to it."

I watched the kids passing in the main corridor. It was almost like a migration, I thought. Calls, colors, and the vitality of spring. Bodies rushing by, intent on other destinations, other pursuits. High school is, in fact, just a stopover on the way to adulthood. What a lot of kids don't realize, unfortunately, is that how they spend those high school years determines the directions they'll take for the rest of their lives. As someone counseling young people, that's the challenge I take up every day: trying to help kids balance their past and present so they can navigate their future. With students like Karl, my job is a breeze; with students like Dani, it wears on your heart. But always, the objective is the same: to help students move forward on their journeys, to equip them with the skills and resources they need to survive, if not thrive.

Ultimately, I guess, what I really want to do is teach them to fly.

At the moment, however, it looked like I was about to engage in some serious wing-clipping.

Mr. Lenzen was heading my way, with Mandy and two other girls trailing in his wake.

Warning. Warning. Clothing police, I thought.

I automatically glanced at Mandy's mid section, but to my relief, it was completely covered by her shirt.

Then I noticed her shoulders.

And her throat.

And the upper half of her chest.

168

Except for skinny little straps that held up a skimpy little top, her skin was bare. The other two girls were likewise enjoying natural air conditioning—not an unreasonable desire for a Minnesotan on a balmy May morning. I mean, after all, we endure at least half the year buried under layers of clothing, our skin turning white and our pores starved for oxygen. Who wouldn't want to shed a winter shell as soon as the air was warm and the sun shining? I know I always did. Even as the girls walked into my office, Mr. Lenzen keeping vigilant guard behind them, I could feel the remnants of my own sun worship—make that sunburn—from the weekend still peeling from my chest.

"I know, I know," Mandy said, as soon as she dropped into a chair. "No spaghetti straps and bare shoulders. But, geez, everyone else does it, and they don't get caught."

"The fact that others don't get caught doing something against the rules isn't a good reason for you to do it," I said, reciting to the girls my canned response to the dress-code complaint. I already knew the next line—"but it isn't fair, Mr. White."

"But it isn't fair, Mr. White!"

"Fair isn't the issue, here. The issue here is playing by the rules. As long as you're at Savage, you have to play by the rules. End of discussion. Do any of you girls have a shirt in your locker you can cover up with?"

After some muttering and mumbling, the three admitted they had shirts in their lockers or could borrow one from a friend.

"Great. You cover up, and we'll get you back to class." I wrote out passes for them to stop by their lockers on their way to class. "Do me a favor," I added. "Save the skin for outside of school. It'll make all of us much happier. You won't be breaking rules, and I won't have to catch you."

The girls took the passes and left. Much as I disliked admitting it, it was true that a lot of students never got collared for dress code violations, which made it very tempting for others to try. In that respect, I realized, high school wasn't any different from the rest of life—there are people everywhere who are tempted to, and do, break the rules of the games when they think they won't get caught.

Is that what Dani's father had thought?

If so, he'd gotten caught in a big way and almost cashed in his chips permanently in payment.

Two more girls appeared in my office doorway, their jeans slung low and their navels well exposed.

"Take a seat," I sighed, waving them in. It was almost enough to make me wish for winter again.

Almost, but not quite.

It was, after all, just about the midpoint of warbler migration, and I still had a Chat and a Kentucky Warbler to find. After our strike-out last night, I had high hopes that the Chat was hanging around in the general area of Dandorff's property, next to Louisville Swamp. The survey tonight would be a perfect opportunity to walk the area, looking for the bird. With a generous dose of luck, maybe I'd even find the Kentucky, too.

And if I were really, really lucky, maybe Rick and I could get enough information from Dani to help Wilson nail down a suspect for Nancy's murder, figure out who Pete Olson had gotten mixed up with, and get some social services in place for Dani and Chris. As far as I was concerned, it was the bottom of the ninth in this game and the bases were loaded. Bringing in just one run wouldn't be nearly enough.

I needed a grand slam.

CHAPTER
TWENTY-EIGHT

By the time I pulled into Dandorff's farmyard that evening, it looked like a parking lot. I was running late, thanks to an extended coaches' meeting after softball practice, so I was one of the last to arrive for the survey, instead of one of the early ones, as I had planned to be. I counted twenty-two vehicles parked in front of the barn and house. I noticed my dad's blue pickup was sitting next to Rick's Trans-Am. I didn't know if Dani had already come and gone after filling Rick in on all the details, but I secretly hoped so. For just a couple of hours, I didn't want to think about Dani and her family. I would be perfectly happy if, in my absence, Rick had stepped up to the plate and been able to knock the ball out of the park.

If he had, it sure wasn't showing on his face when I rounded the corner of the house to join the crowd of people in the back yard. He was standing near an old clothesline pole and, as soon as he saw me, waved me over to him. Beside him were my dad and Dani, who was whispering with Bridget. Karl and Arne moved through the crowd, giving instructions for the survey and counting off teams of people to take the positions that were numbered on a large blown-up map of Dandorff's property that someone had propped up against the back porch. Looking around, I recognized a few local birders I'd met over the years, along with some people who looked familiar to me from the council meeting on Tuesday night. Ray and Janssen were there, too, chatting with Dandorff on the back porch. The sun was dipping to the

west and the air was still, clear and warm, which bode well for birding—without rain or wind, the birds should be active and easy to
count. As long as the various groups of participants moved quietly
along the trails that Karl and Arne had marked, the birds shouldn't
be disturbed or startled from their grounds, either.

All in all, it looked to be a good night for birding, and I couldn't
help but be optimistic I'd find something out here tonight. A Louisiana
Waterthrush or the Yellow-breasted Chat would be nice.

"Hey, Dad," I said, clapping him on the shoulder, "thanks for
coming. It's been a while since we've birded together. Rick, Dani—
sorry I'm so late. The coaches' meeting went a bit longer than I'd
anticipated." I nodded at Bridget. "That swing is really coming along,
Bridget. We're going to work on straightening it out, right?"

"You bet, Coach."

"Dani and I had a chance to talk already, Bob," Rick said. "I
think after the survey, she and I are going to go talk to Wilson together. There are definitely some things we both think he should hear. Do
you want to come with us?"

I looked from Rick to Dani. "Do you want me to?"

Dani didn't have to answer. I could see the thinly veiled anxiety
on her face.

"I'll tag along. Is Chris still here?" I looked around but didn't see
him in the yard.

"No, he had to go. He started a new job, and he doesn't want to
miss work," Dani explained.

"I promised Chris I'd get her home safe and sound," Rick added.
"Later, after the survey and after our visit with Wilson."

"Sounds like a plan," I agreed.

Karl had worked his way over to our group and was handing out
notebooks for us to keep track of the birds we saw. "I need this group
to take the trail that skirts Louisville Swamp. If you go around the
corner of the barn, you'll see a wide pathway that angles off to the
right. That's the trail," Karl said. "In about a hundred yards, the trail

splits, so your group will have to split, too, so we can cover all the positions we decided on during our meeting on Sunday night. I just need to know who's going where, so I can mark it on our master map, and we can track where the noise is the loudest."

He handed a small walkie-talkie to both me and my dad. "When you reach your positions—and we've marked them all with flags on the trails so you can't miss them—call in so we know when all thirteen teams are in place. Then, when we're all set, I'll crank up the volume on the sound system we've got set up behind the barn to simulate an outdoor concert. I'll do a countdown on the walkie-talkie so you know when I'll be turning it up. After ten minutes, walk back and note what birds are still around. Any questions?"

"Who's going with me?" I asked. "Dani?"

"Actually, I thought I'd go with your dad, Mr. White. Is that okay? He said he has an extra pair of binoculars that I could use, if I wanted."

My dad covered a smile with his hand and adjusted his baseball cap; he'd obviously been practicing his best charming grandfather-type routine on Dani, and she'd lapped it up.

"Sure," I told her. "He's one of the best birders here, you know." I lowered my voice to a deep rumble. "You have chosen wisely, Dani."

"Bob White, is that you?"

I turned around to find Bernie from Little Six standing behind me.

"It is you!" She clapped her hands together. "I thought I recognized that red head of yours from across the yard. My hair used to be that same color, you know."

"So I've heard," I told her. I introduced her to my dad and Dani. She remembered Rick from last night.

"You poor thing," she said to Dani. "I just heard from some of the other people here that it was your father who was shot last night. I was right there, dear. He had everyone helping him right away. How is he doing?"

Dani shifted the tiniest bit closer to my father. Bernie was so intent, I figured it scared Dani off a bit. I knew how she felt. I got the distinct impression myself that Bernie would mother anyone to death given half the chance.

"He's doing okay," Dani answered. "The doctors said he's going to be in the hospital for a while before he can come home."

Rick and I exchanged a look.

Unless he doesn't come home, I silently added, because he has a new address at the state prison.

"Well, I live right out here in Jordan, and if you need anything, you just give me a call." Bernie took the notebook that Dani was holding and flipped it open to the inside cover. She fished in her jacket pocket and produced a pen that she then used to write her name and phone number on the cover.

"Here you go, dear." Bernie handed it back to Dani. "You call me, all right?"

Dani looked at the notebook, then at Bernie. Her chin quivered a little.

I started to panic.

I hadn't brought tissues with me.

"Which birding survey team are you on tonight, Bernie?" Rick asked.

Dani's chin firmed up. She didn't cry. Rick to the rescue once again.

At this rate, I was going to owe him a case of beer by the weekend.

"I'm birding with you, Officer Cook. You and Bob." Bernie fluttered her eyelashes at both of us. "Wait till I tell the girls I spent an evening with two young hunks. They're going to want to take up birding, too."

I felt so . . . cheep.

CHAPTER
TWENTY-NINE

Bridget left our little group to go help Karl operate the sound system. While I tested the walkie-talkie, Bernie entertained my dad, Rick, and Dani with stories about the birding weekend we met, and how she thought that Luce and I had just been the cutest couple she had ever seen.

"I told your son that he should marry that gal," Bernie confided to my dad, though there was nothing confidential in her tone. Everyone within twenty yards of her could hear every word, I was sure. I caught Dani sneaking glances at me. She was probably wondering about this girlfriend of mine that she'd never heard about. My dad, charmer and tease that he was, kept egging Bernie on for more details about the weekend I met Luce.

No doubt, I'd now be hearing those details again and again whenever Luce and I had dinner with my parents.

I shuddered to think what Lily might do with them.

"Okay, everybody," Karl announced from the back porch of the Dandorff farmhouse. He'd finished writing in the names of the various survey team members at each numbered position on the map. "Here's what we've got. Check and make sure I've got your name up here. I want to be able to track incoming calls from the walkie-talkies by team number so we can monitor the movements of birds and birders alike." He paused to flash his big grin. "And then you can take a hike. To your point on the map, that is."

A few chuckles followed his announcement. All the birders checked their assignments and left the yard, heading off in different directions to their designated observation points.

Rick, Bernie, and I were about ten minutes down our trail, having already made the split from my dad and Dani, when I heard the sharp *chink* of the Louisiana Waterthrush. I stopped on the path and listened.

"What?" Bernie whispered. "What do you hear?"

I pointed silently towards the small stream off to my left, and we all lifted our binoculars to our eyes to search the undergrowth. The bird continued to sing.

"There, on the ground," I said. "In front of that old tree trunk."

I wasn't particularly surprised to see the warbler. Though it was typically one of the more rare ones to find, I'd been successful in locating it the last two years in this general area. Rick and Bernie, on the other hand, had both mentioned they hadn't seen one in several years, so we took the time to watch the bird through our binoculars, noting its white throat and eye stripe that distinguished it from the Northern Waterthrush.

As we listened to the warbler singing, it suddenly occurred to me that the tune we were hearing might, if OEI built its complex on this land, become a swan song, signaling the end of the Waterthrush's familiarity with the area. As accustomed as I was to birding in this part of the Minnesota River valley, it hadn't really struck me till now that the only thing between preserving this space and tearing it all up was the vote of four people.

Granted, those people had been elected by their constituents to make decisions that served the best interests of the community as a whole. At the same time, though, those four individuals were dependent on the information, input and concern supplied by others. Nor could anyone completely put aside his or her own prejudices or bias about certain goals. Now, as I walked the trail on Dandorff's land and heard the Waterthrush call, thinking it could be the last May I'd hear it, I sent a silent, heartfelt, thank-you to Karl for bringing the public's attention to this rich resource of habitat and land. I could only hope that it had not come too late.

We started moving again, and Bernie took a good lead, leaving Rick and me a little privacy to talk.

"I think that Wilson will be able to do something for Dani about her living situation," Rick said. "Even if a judge lets Olson out on bail, I think that given the fact that she's afraid of her dad and that she may have valuable information for a case against him, Wilson will work to move her out of the house for her own safety. Question is: where? If the juvenile authorities get involved, I don't know that they'll go for having her move in with Chris right now. And I don't think a foster home is the answer, either."

He stopped to listen for birds, then shook his head. "Thought I heard something."

I thought I heard something, too. A humming noise.

Rick and I both looked at Bernie's back ahead of us on the trail. "She's humming," Rick whispered.

"It's Bernie," I said at the same time.

"Should we say something?"

"Nah," I said. "She's not loud enough to bother the birds. And I doubt she can hear us talking over it. Works for me."

Rick picked up where he'd left off. "I don't know that I go for Dani moving in with Chris right now, either, Bob, to tell you the truth. We've still got your shooter to identify. Until Pete Olson is up to talking with us, we can't be sure he's the guilty party for that one. And we still don't know for sure the reason behind the attack. So whether your shooter targeted you because you'd been at Chris's place, or just because you were in the area, either way, I don't think it's safe for Dani. Although," he paused a beat, "if Chris has already been working with a social worker about Dani moving into his home, we might be able to pull something off. Maybe get them both relocated temporarily." He shrugged, then lifted his binos to his eyes.

"What do you see?" I asked, scanning the trees ahead of us.

"The Chat," he answered.

I raised my binos in the direction he was looking, but couldn't find it.

"I lied," he said.

I dropped my binos and smacked him in the arm. "I should have gone with my dad. Dani really did choose wisely."

"It's about time," Rick muttered as we started walking again. "I know why she hadn't come forward with the information she had, but it wasn't a good decision for anyone. It let too much time pass after the fact, time for any leads or evidence to get cold. Even now, she can't positively identify the car she saw following her mother's. It's just a scrap of a lead, but if it was Dani's dad, it might be enough for Wilson to use to push Olson into a confession. Her being at Chris's trailer for the whole night will help more, since it gives Chris the alibi he needs."

"Are you tag-alongs coming?" Bernie stood in the middle of the trail about twenty paces ahead of us, hands on plump hips. "I found the flag that nice young Karl said would mark our listening point. It's right here."

Next to Bernie stood a bright orange traffic cone, a pole sticking out of its top with a little American flag flying from its tip.

Karl had obviously been here. Thank you, Mr. President.

I listened for a moment, but the birds seemed to have gone quiet. I called in to Karl and told him we were at our position. He said we were the last team on site and that the sound system would be on in a minute.

"Sixty seconds, people," Karl's voice announced. "I'll count down the last ten seconds, so keep your walkie-talkies on."

I clipped the little black box back on my pocket. Bernie found a log, sat down on it and started quietly humming again.

"I wonder if there's anyone else who knows Dani was at the trailer that night," I said to Rick, careful to keep my voice low. "Call me paranoid, but it seems like there's always someone else who knows things about last weekend before we hear about it."

"Well, if they didn't before, they do now."

I looked at Rick.

He wasn't happy.

"Dani was so nervous, or so relieved, to tell me about being with Chris and seeing the car, that she blurted it out almost as soon as I arrived," he explained, his voice as low as mine. "Unfortunately, I didn't get here as early as I had wanted to, either, so by the time I found her in the back yard, there was a crowd of people around." He kicked at a branch lying across the trail. "At least ten other people must have heard her tell me."

I glanced at Bernie and nodded in her direction. She smiled back at me.

"That's how Bernie knew who Dani was, isn't it? People were talking about the Olsons after they overheard her in the yard."

Rick tugged on his ear stud. "That's my guess. And now it's a mess. In a murder investigation, you sure don't want everyone privy to details, Bob. It can compromise evidence or testimony. Most especially, you don't want the identity of any witnesses to be common knowledge, since it puts their lives in danger."

He paused and gave me a warning look. "Don't forget that Pete Olson was shot last night, Bob. Who's to say that if word got out that Dani was a witness to her dad killing her mother, that whoever went after Olson last night wouldn't come after Dani?"

Despite the warmth of the evening, a shiver tripped down my spine.

"Think about it, Bob. If each of the people here tonight who heard Dani talking about the car told even one or two friends what they heard, you can imagine how fast that information is going to fly."

The shiver became a definite chill.

"Ten!" Karl's voice began the countdown.

"So, Dani may have just put herself right in the sights of a killer."

"Got it in one, Bob."

"Six!"

"You two are sure talking a lot for people who are supposed to be listening," Bernie complained from her seat on the log.

"Two!

I realized the humming had stopped.

"One!"

No music screamed from the speakers.

Instead, there was another noise.

A crack.

Of a rifle.

"Get down!" I shouted, diving for Bernie.

CHAPTER THIRTY

Rick was next to me in the dirt. I could feel Bernie under my arm, her body heaving as she tried to catch the breath I'd knocked out of her.

"Stay down!" Rick ordered. He raised himself up on one elbow and pulled out his cell phone from inside his jacket while I ripped the walkie-talkie off my pants pocket and hit the send button. In the same instant, the sound system blared music through the woods.

"Somebody's shooting out here!" I shouted into the transmitter. "Get everybody down! And turn off the music! Now!"

Rick was shouting into his phone, too. "We've got a shooting! Possible injuries! Get me backup, ambulances!"

"We don't know if anyone's been hit," I practically panted as the adrenaline surged through my body. Man, I hate that feeling.

"I'm not waiting to find out. We need backup, and we need it now."

The talkie buzzed in my hand and Karl's voice, shaken and shocked, came out of the box. "I turned it off, Mr. White. What do we do now?"

"Sit tight. Rick's called 911. Help is on the way. Everybody needs to report in. Got that?" I hoped desperately that all the survey teams had kept their walkie-talkies on, as Karl had instructed before his countdown. "Everyone call in, so Karl knows you're okay. Stay where you are and call in."

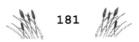

181

"Can I come up now?" a little voice under my arm said.

Geez. I'd almost forgotten that Bernie was pinned under one side of my body.

I lifted my arm off her back and rolled onto my side. She rolled in the opposite direction and stared back at me.

Her eyes were huge in her face. Dirt and leaves were stuck in her silver hair.

"Does this happen to you a lot?"

"Does what happen to me?"

"Shootings. Last night. Today."

And the day before yesterday, too, if anyone was counting. Three in a row. If I'd been playing a one-armed bandit, it would have been a jackpot.

Funny. I didn't feel like I had scored.

"Not usually," I told her.

"Good," she said. She smiled. "I'd hate to have to give up bird-ing with you just because people are always shooting around you. A little excitement is nice, but I'm getting too old for a roll in the dirt. Even with a handsome devil like you. When can I get up?"

"Not yet," Rick told her from where he was lying on the ground, too. "Not till I say."

On the walkie-talkie, teams were reporting in. I had no idea who was on which team, nor did I have any idea where their positions were located in relation to our own.

At the moment, I didn't care. The only thing that I did care about was listening for the sound of my dad's voice, telling us he and Dani were okay.

He didn't check in.

Four more teams called Karl.

Still no Dad.

It suddenly occurred to me what those three shootings in a row had in common.

An Olson.

I'd been targeted after seeing Chris.

Pete Olson was shot in the casino.

Dani was here in the woods.

I felt the adrenaline spiking again.

"Come on, Dad," I whispered, prayed, pleaded. "Come on."

"We're here." My father's voice finally came through the walkie-talkie in my hand. My breath blew out in a rush of relief.

"But we need help," he said. "Dani's been shot."

CHAPTER THIRTY-ONE

Rick was up and running before I could scramble to my feet.

I didn't even think twice.

I took off after him.

Hot on his heels, I raced back down the trail to the split, then out towards the position my dad and Dani had been assigned. If somebody wanted to shoot me, let him shoot, I thought, hurdling bushes and slapping branches aside as I rushed through the woods. All week I'd worried about Dani's safety and now, when she was with my own father, birding in the woods, she'd been hurt. And there was no way that was a freak accident. It wasn't hunting season. Not to mention that firearms were prohibited in Louisville Swamp at any time of year.

Like that would make any difference to someone set on going on a shooting spree.

Just like the stupid gun ban signs at Little Six hadn't kept someone from shooting Pete Olson last night.

Fact: Almost three dozen birders were out on these trails right now, but only Dani had been shot.

Fact: Only one shot had been fired. At Dani.

Conclusion: Dani was the target.

Shit.

My lungs burning, I spotted my dad sitting on the trail with his arms wrapped around Dani. She was propped up in his lap, and he was holding a wadded piece of clothing tightly against her left

shoulder. Her face was pale, but she was conscious and responding to my dad's conversation.

"She's going to be fine," my dad assured me when I reached them. I sat on my haunches in front of Dani and stroked her hair back from her face. I refilled my lungs with air. I could feel Rick hovering just behind me. He was on his phone again, giving the emergency dispatcher explicit directions for finding us.

"This is one tough customer," my dad said, giving Dani a gentle squeeze. "She got nicked on the shoulder. Didn't even pass out."

He gave me one of those parental looks I recognized from my childhood, a look that said "something is seriously wrong here." For Dani's benefit, though, he said out loud, "Some idiot's out in the woods taking target practice."

"Yeah, we heard the shot," Rick told him. "Bob called Karl to warn everyone else, and I called 911. We've got emergency people on the way."

He nudged me over with his foot and knelt beside Dani, checking her pulse and then her pupils. "You're doing okay, Dani. As soon as the paramedics get here, we'll take care of that shoulder." He switched his attention to my dad. "By any chance—any long shot—did you see anyone?"

My dad shook his head. "We were just listening for the birds, Rick. That's all. I heard the shot and pushed Dani down. And then we were on the ground, wadding up my jacket to hold against her shoulder. I didn't see a thing."

"I saw a Chat."

I was so startled to hear Dani's voice that what she said escaped me for a second. "What?"

"I saw a Chat. Your dad said you'd be so jealous, Mr. White."

I looked at Dani sitting in the circle of my father's arms. My dad was wrong—at the moment, the last thing on my mind was being jealous. But he was right about Dani—she was a tough customer. She'd survived growing up in a dysfunctional household only to have her

mother murdered, her dad nearly killed, and now, she herself had taken a bullet.

Yet here she was, talking about a bird, holding it together while we waited for help.

I didn't know what to feel first—pride in her coping skills, awe for her courage, or utter amazement at her resiliency. I did know, however, what I felt second: fury at someone with a gun.

Someone who'd aimed it at Dani.

But even as I steamed, Rick's questions for my dad came to mind. Why would my dad have seen anything? There were a lot of woods out here, and the foliage was getting thick enough to hide anyone. Whoever had taken the shot had known exactly what they were doing and where they were aiming, otherwise the chances of Dani getting hit by a stray bullet in a wildlife refuge were beyond astronomical. Certainly Rick didn't think this had been a random act of violence by some crazy person in the swamp.

Then I realized what he and my dad were doing.

They didn't want Dani to panic.

Knowing she'd been an intentional target wouldn't keep her calm. She needed to sit quietly till the ambulance crew got here. That's why my dad had said it was some idiot in the woods. Rick had played along, and he was trying to piece together information without Dani guessing the truth of what had just happened.

That somebody had tried to kill her.

Since my dad hadn't seen or heard anyone moving in the woods, that could only mean that the shooter was in place when Dad and Dani got to their assigned position. Which also meant that the shooter knew they were going to be there.

Which, finally, meant that the shooter had seen Karl's map on the back porch of the Dandorff farmhouse.

Conclusion: whoever had taken a shot at Dani had been in the yard.

And why would anyone try to kill Dani?

I could think of only one reason.

She was a witness.

That same chill was back in my spine, only worse.

A lot worse.

Because I suddenly realized that the odds had just dropped pre-cipitously that Pete Olson had killed his wife. The real killer was here at the farm, and he was trying to clean up after himself now that he knew Dani had the one clue to who he was.

I looked at Dani sitting with my dad. If my father hadn't been so quick to react and knocked her down as soon as he heard the crack of the rifle, would she even be alive?

And if Karl had started the music exactly when he'd said he was going to, instead of a few seconds late, would my dad have even heard that rifle crack?

The crack that would have been masked by the music blast?

It hit me like a lead balloon: the shooter had a walkie-talkie.

How else would he have known when that music was supposed to start? The music that he had planned on covering the sound of the rifle shot.

The rifle shot that would kill Dani.

Dani—the one witness to Nancy Olson's murder.

Rick was already ahead of me. He was back on the walkie-talkie with Karl, telling him to make sure none of the birders left the farm until everyone was interviewed by the police. At almost the same moment, the first emergency personnel came running up the trail. Things were happening fast, and I backed away from Dani and my dad to give the paramedics room. Two officers questioned me, Rick was saying something to Karl on the walkie-talkie, the medics were bandaging Dani, and I saw blood on my dad's hand and shirt. More police were in the woods off the trail, pointing and searching, but apparently nothing was turning up. The medics put Dani on a stretch-er and took off down the trail, my dad with them. He yelled back to me, saying he'd see me at the emergency room.

"We've got to talk to Karl," Rick said. "Find out who had the walkie-talkies."

"And a rifle?"

"Yeah," he said. "And a rifle."

"Not exactly standard equipment for a birder," I noted.

"Not exactly," he agreed.

On the way back to the farmhouse, Rick told me he'd called Wilson when the paramedics had taken Dani and filled him in on what had been going on since he'd arrived at Dandorff's and spoken with Dani.

"He's on his way here now, and he is definitely not happy, I can tell you that. I have no doubt I'll be getting a reaming for not cluing him in as soon as I knew about Dani being at the trailer on Friday night, or about Dani and the car, not to mention Dani and the gun."

He shook his head in self-disgust.

"I am such an idiot. It never occurred to me that Dani might not be safe here this evening. I mean, geez, all these people around, just birding. Our prime suspect in the hospital. Wilson close to making an arrest. Mistake, mistake, mistake! The kind of mistake that gets someone killed."

"She's going to be okay, Rick." I definitely felt as stupid and negligent as he did, but figured it wasn't the time for a personal pity party. Dani wasn't out of the woods, yet.

Well, actually, by now, she probably was. Those medics could run even with a stretcher between them.

"What did Dani tell you about the gun, Rick?"

He shrugged as we jogged down the trail. "She didn't know where her mom got it and I didn't find any records of a sale to Nancy. But Dani insisted no one else knew about it, which means that, more than likely, whoever killed Nancy took the gun, since it's missing. I figured Olson had it stashed away somewhere. Why take the gun? One of two reasons: it's either the murder weapon or it can somehow be used to identify the murderer. Maybe both."

"In which case," I continued his line of reasoning, "Nancy got the gun from her killer, meaning she knew her killer and was even on good enough terms to borrow a gun from him. Or her."

"Not a 'her,' Bob. Definitely a 'him.' It's very unlikely that a woman could have hauled Nancy all the way to the creek from her car."

"Yeah, I know. It's an old habit from grad school—inclusive language. Looks good on paper but sounds stupid when you speak it."

Speaking of paper, Karl met us at the edge of the farmyard, holding a notebook.

"Here you go, Officer Cook. I made a list of all the people at each position and checked off the names that were called in after the gunshot. I also marked who took the walkie-talkies. They're all accounted for."

Rick took the notebook and I looked over his shoulder to read it.

"You're sure this is everyone?" Rick tapped the page.

"You bet. I wrote the teams down as we assigned them before everybody headed out."

"Where are Dandorff's, Ray's and Janssen's names?" I asked, remembering seeing them in the crowd.

"They didn't go out to survey, Mr. White."

"They didn't?"

"Where are they?" Rick practically jumped at Karl, startling him into taking a couple steps backward. He grasped the boy's shoulders in his hands, his eyes intent on Karl's face. "I need to know where they are. Where they were after the rest of us went into the woods. Did they take walkie-talkies? It's important, Karl."

"I don't know, Officer Cook."

Karl laced his hands behind his head and shifted his weight from foot to foot. It was the first time I'd ever seen him distraught, but I could tell he was trying hard to concentrate, to remember.

"After everyone left for their positions, they talked a little bit here in the yard and then walked toward the barn. I don't know if they had walkie-talkies. We had a ton of them lying on the porch for people to use. Maybe they took one. I don't know for certain. Then I guess Mr. Ray and Mr. Janssen left, because I heard some car engines. Bridget and I were sitting on the porch, waiting for everyone to say they were at their positions, so we could turn on the sound system."

A slow blush crept up Karl's cheeks. "That's why I was a couple of seconds late turning on the speakers. I—well—I was kissing Bridget in between counting down and when I got to 'one,' it took a little longer to kiss her than I'd meant it to. I'm sorry."

"Don't be," I told him. "Your getting distracted that extra second or two may have saved Dani's life."

"Yeah?" He stopped shifting his weight and smiled tentatively. "Okay. That's good, then. Anyway," he resumed, "I didn't see anyone else around here until after you called in and told me about the gunshot and that everyone should report in. Sometime after that, I noticed Mr. Dandorff coming out of the barn. I told him what was going on, and he stayed here with me and Bridget until the police came. I think he's in the house, now."

Rick stared across the yard at the barn. "Is there a back door to that barn?"

What was he thinking? That Dandorff had slipped out the back, tracked down Dani and taken a shot at her?

Dandorff?

"I don't know, Officer Cook."

Rick walked over to the barn, through the big open front door and, after a few minutes, came back.

"There's a door," he said. "And it leads right into the woods."

CHAPTER THIRTY-TWO

The sound of tires spinning on gravel in front of the house caught our attention. A car door slammed, and seconds later, Detective Wilson walked around the side of the house.

"I passed the ambulance on the way here," he said when he got out of the car. He was about my height, I noticed, maybe ten years older. "Dani's going to be okay, I take it."

"Yeah," Rick said. "Thanks to Bob's dad. He pushed her down when he heard the shot."

"You are in such deep yogurt with me, Cook." Wilson glanced at Karl. I expected that his word choice might have been different if Karl hadn't been there.

"My fault, Detective," I volunteered. I'd brought Rick into this mess, after all, feeding him tips for Wilson. "I should have been passing along to you what Dani has been telling me for the last few days, but I wasn't sure—I mean, I didn't know—"

"Let's go from here," he interrupted me. "We'll do the reprimands later. What've we got?"

Rick showed him Karl's list and explained how we couldn't account for the whereabouts of Dandorff, Ray, and Janssen at the time of the shooting. From where we stood in the middle of the back yard, we pointed out the different paths the survey groups had taken and Karl showed him the large map on the porch with the marked positions. All the other birders were now milling around the yard, talking

excitedly in small groups, doubtless speculating about what was going on. Wilson directed the other officers on the scene to take statements from everyone, while he headed for the house to interview Dandorff.

I turned to Rick. "I want to go to the hospital. I need to see Dani."

"Go," he said. "I'll catch up with you later."

Night was falling when I pulled out of Dandorff's drive onto the county road. The more I tried to reassure myself that Wilson had to be on the verge of solving Nancy's murder and getting Dani out of danger, the less I believed it. For the past few days, every time I thought the detective was just a hair from identifying the murderer, more leads had popped up. So far, he didn't seem any closer to making an arrest than he had been on Saturday afternoon after my mom found Nancy floating in the swamp.

Except now, the ante had gone way up. Dani had been shot. And even though Rick and I were both convinced that this shooter and Nancy's killer were one and the same, we had no way to prove it. All we had was the fact that whoever took aim at Dani tonight had to have been in the farmyard with us, and of all those people, only three were unaccounted for when the rifle cracked: Dandorff, Ray, and Janssen.

They all had stakes in the OEI deal.

I pressed my gas pedal closer to the floorboards.

Using Karl's map, any one of the three men could have found his way to a vantage point from where he could have lined Dani up in his sights. I was sure both Dandorff and Ray knew how to shoot: they'd lived on farms all their lives. I didn't know about Janssen, but chances were good he'd bagged his quota of deer over the years along with half of the male population of Minnesota. I remembered he had a gun rack in his truck.

More adrenaline poured through my veins.

My speedometer registered higher.

One of these guys—men who were practically pillars of the community—had sunk so low as to try to kill a child to cover up a murder.

A murder over a piece of land and the money it would produce.
Something was seriously wrong here, as my father would say.

I thought of Dani in my father's arms, her shoulder bleeding.

I wanted to shoot someone myself.

Instead, I got pulled over.

Adrenaline, I realized too late, goes straight to your gas pedal.

Damn.

"I'm on my way to the emergency room, officer," I shouted out
my window, as soon as the patrolman was close enough to hear, thinking how lame it had to sound to him. "A student of mine was shot at
the Dandorff property—"

"I heard about it," he interrupted. "I'm giving you an escort."
And he went back to his cruiser.

For a second, I thought I was imagining things. No ticket? An
escort? The patrolman got back in his car and pulled in front of me,
lights flashing. How did he know?

Rick.

Rick had alerted the posse.

And all the officer had to do was look at my vanity plate to know
it was me.

BRRDMAN.

I took off after the squad car and flew through the night.

CHAPTER
THIRTY-THREE

Barely five minutes later, I waved off my escort and parked near the hospital emergency room entrance. The doors slid open for me, and the first person I saw in the waiting area was my dad.

"She's in surgery," he told me. "She's going to do fine, Bob."

I collapsed in a chair and realized that Chris Olson was sitting beside me.

"I just got here, too," he said. "Your dad called me on the way here with Dani in the ambulance."

"Dani asked me to call him," Dad explained. "She was a real trooper, I'm telling you. Didn't complain once all the way here."

I noticed a police officer sitting across the room. Chris nodded in his direction. "My buddy for the day. Courtesy of Officer Cook."

Rick had thought of everything.

"I thought I'd go see how my dad's doing, since I'm here," Chris told me. "Want to come?"

I glanced at my father.

"Go," he said. "Maybe the doctor'll be done with Dani by the time you get back and you can see her."

We took the elevator up to the fourth floor and asked to see Pete Olson. The nurse recognized Chris from earlier in the day and showed us to his father's room.

"He's resting comfortably," she said. "A little conversation would be okay, but don't tire him out."

 194

A maze of tubes hung near the bed, and I got my first look at Dani's father. On Eddie's surveillance tapes, Pete had looked to be mid-forties, balding and pale. In a hospital bed, recovering from a gunshot wound, he looked a lot older than mid-forties, though he was still balding, and really pale. He was also a larger man than I had expected, probably about five-ten and over two hundred pounds. From what Dani had told me about him, I had imagined him to be small and hen-pecked, weak and meek. The big guy in the bed surprised me.

"Hi, Dad," Chris said, dropping into the chair beside the bed.

Pete's eyes opened.

"I brought a friend."

Dani's dad looked me over.

"I'm Bob White, Dani's counselor at school."

He closed his eyes again and seemed to drift asleep. I told Chris I'd be in the emergency waiting room with my dad and left, but when I got back downstairs, my dad was gone.

The receptionist behind the counter waved at me. "Mr. White? Your father's in with Dani. She's resting right now. The doctor says you can come in, but he asks that you don't wake her."

I found my dad behind Curtain Number Five in the emergency room suite, sitting in a chair beside Dani's bed.

"She's doing great," he whispered. "It really was just a graze. There'll be a police guard here for her anytime now. Detective Wilson called the desk to tell the doctor that Dani gets security till further notice."

"Wise move," I whispered back. "I already blew it once, trying to keep her safe. He's got to do a better job than I did."

"Don't beat yourself up, Bob. You couldn't have known."

I knew he was right, but it didn't help much. From the minute Dani had asked me to help Chris, I'd appointed myself her protector. And where had that gotten her?

In the hospital with a gunshot wound.

"I expect her father will be pretty shook up when he finds out," Dad said.

I thought of the big guy sleeping upstairs with his son watching beside him. "It might be a while before he knows about it," I reminded Dad. "Pete Olson isn't exactly in the best of parenting shapes right now."

Then again, he wasn't in a casino, either, so maybe there was hope for Dani's father yet.

"You know, until an hour ago, I was thinking that Pete Olson was the one who'd killed Nancy." I told him about the trip Rick and I had made to Little Six and the tapes Eddie had run for us.

"It looked pretty damning," I said, "seeing a fat envelope in Olson's hands just hours after his wife was murdered and knowing he'd been throwing money around this week. Combine that with Dani's suspicions about the car she saw and possibly violence between her parents, and it wasn't too much of a leap. But Pete Olson wasn't there tonight, he didn't hear her talking about seeing the car, so that means someone else wants to get rid of her as a witness to a murder."

"And that person is also Nancy's killer?"

"I'd bet the farm on it. That is, I would if I had one." I paused. "Dad, there were only three people there tonight who could have shot at Dani: Dandorff, Ray, or Janssen. And Dandorff has more motive than anyone, Dad. Maybe Ray would make money selling his property if OEI moves in, and Janssen could use the deal as a political coup, but Dandorff is the one who's taking it to the bank. He's going to make a pile of money on that property."

Dad shook his head. "No, he's not, son. Not anymore."

"What?"

"He's not going to sell the property to OEI."

That couldn't be right. I was at the council meeting on Tuesday, for cripe's sake. Dandorff told me his plans. Everything was set to go, including him. He was going to head south and pay for his grandkids' college education with the proceeds of the sale.

My dad was wrong.

"He's changed his mind," Dad said. "He told me tonight before the survey. He didn't want Karl to feel his work was for naught, so he didn't say anything to anyone. He figured whatever the survey turned up would be good supportive material for what he wants to do with the land." He clasped my shoulder with his hand and grinned. "He's going to deed it to the state for a preserve, Bob."

I had to sit down. "When did this happen? Just two nights ago, he—"

"My fault, Bob, if you can call it a fault. I'd rather call it serendipity. A happy coincidence," he clarified.

"I know what it means," I snapped, not meaning to. "Sorry."

"No offense taken." He sat down next to me in a chair identical to the one I sat in: standard emergency room issue of boxy wood frame with blue-patterned seat and back cushions. "It's been a rough week."

"You got that right."

"After you were at the house on Sunday night for dinner, I got to thinking about Dandorff's land. The more I thought about it, the more I couldn't bear it that he was selling it away for development, instead of making it a preserve. I called him on Monday, and we had dinner yesterday evening. He's still hurting from his wife's passing, Bob. He had thought the best thing was to cut the bonds he had with the land where they'd lived together for so long, so he wouldn't see her and think about her every time he turned around. I told him a preserve in her name was a better idea—he could celebrate her life forever and still move away from the sad reminders if he wanted. He said he'd think about it, but he'd already decided when I saw him tonight. He's telling the council at their meeting tomorrow."

I was stunned.

Speechless, even.

It was over.

The OEI complex wasn't going to happen.

Ever.

Or at least, not on Dandorff's land. And even though nobody else would know about it until tomorrow, OEI's proposal was now a thing of the past, and everybody involved with it was done.

Except for whoever had shot Dani.

He still thought the game was on.

So, who was the shooter?

Ray or Janssen?

I needed to call Rick and tell him it wasn't Dandorff.

"Mr. White?"

Dad and I both turned to see who was standing beside the room curtain. It was Chris.

"My dad's asking for you," he said. "It's about an envelope."

CHAPTER
THIRTY-FOUR

There was money in the envelope," Pete Olson told me, his voice slurring a little from his medications. "The guy had approached me before, a couple months ago, saying if I could get Nancy to vote for the proposal, he had a payoff for me."

He dragged in a long breath. The tubes attached to his arm swayed a little. Chris had told me that his dad wanted to speak with me alone, so he'd stayed in the emergency room with my father and Dani, and I'd come up on the elevator by myself.

"He trusts you because he knows Dani does," Chris had explained. "He says it's important, what he wants to tell you. I think he knows the police want to arrest him for my mom's murder."

Lying in his hospital bed, Olson closed his eyes briefly before continuing.

"I had a lot of debts. You probably figured that out. It sounded good, but no way could I convince Nancy to change her mind, so I told the guy to forget it. Then, Sunday night, some guy I've never seen before slips me an envelope. The next minute, he's gone."

He took another breath and looked me in the eye. "I opened it up and there they were—a pile of big bills. The guy was gone. I kept the money. Bought Dani a bed. Played some cards. I figured Nancy was dead anyway. If someone wanted to give me the money, I'd take it."

"Someone thought you'd killed your wife, Mr. Olson. It was a payoff."

He made a ghost of a shrug. "The money would help. There was no one to give it back to, anyway."

I felt sick to my stomach.

"I didn't kill my wife. I took the money, but I didn't kill her."

For a million reasons, I realized I hated this man. He'd virtually abandoned Dani and Chris, kept the family scrambling for basic living expenses because of his gambling habit, practically handed his own son over to the police for a murder he hadn't committed, and failed to keep his children safe. And now, he seemed more intent on explaining to me why he'd kept an envelope of cash that was clearly intended to be blood money rather than asking about his daughter's physical condition in the emergency room downstairs.

Even worse, he didn't seem to be aware of what Dani had gone through emotionally in the last few days—not only the grieving for her mother, but the growing suspicion and fear of her own father. If he hadn't already been laid up in a hospital bed, I had the awful feeling I might have put him there myself.

Did I care?

"I need to get back to Dani." I could speak fairly clearly through clenched teeth, I discovered.

"Sure." He closed his eyes and dozed off again.

I went back to the emergency room and leaned against the wall in Dani's curtained cubicle. I noted that the bandage covering her left shoulder already had Chris's autograph on it.

"Are you going to sign it, too?"

I hadn't realized her eyes had opened.

"Hey, Mr. White."

"Hey, yourself. How are you doing?"

"Tired. I want to go to Chris's trailer, Mr. White."

"I know you do."

I smiled, painfully aware I couldn't reassure her about anything at this point. "We'll ask the doctor about releasing you. See what he says. Right now, you rest a little more, okay?"

I touched her hand on the bed. "You're a champ, Dani. You're a real champ."

"Hey," she said, after I had started for the door. "I need to tell you, I saw the car at Mr. Dandorff's when they were putting me in the ambulance."

"What car?"

"You know—the one I saw following my mom last Friday night."

Both Chris and my dad sat up straighter in their chairs. I came back to Dani's bedside and covered her hand with mine, my eyes locked on her face. "Dani, are you sure?"

"I'm sure." With her right hand, she gingerly touched the bandage over her wound. "When I saw it tonight, I remembered it—it had this old-fashioned . . . like . . . little statue on its hood. It was the car, Mr. White."

I gripped her hand beneath my own.

"Your dad told me that the really good birders notice details other people miss. He said that was why you were such a good birder and a good counselor—because you see and hear what other people don't."

I hoped she was right, because right now, my head was spinning through all the conversations and visual memories I could call up from the last five days, ever since the moment my mom discovered Nancy Olson's body floating in the marsh. If Dani was right—and my gut was telling me she was—then the car she had seen tonight was the car that her mother's murderer had driven to and from the scene of the crime. But if she'd seen the car after the shooting, after both Janssen and Ray had already left the farm according to Karl, it couldn't have been either of their cars Dani had seen on her way to the ambulance.

That left only one possibility: Dani had seen Dandorff's car.

And that meant I finally knew who had killed Nancy Olson and dumped her in the stream at Murphy-Hanrehan.

I was already moving across the room when I stopped and turned back one more time. "I've got to make some phone calls, Dani." I wanted to tell her I knew who had killed her mom, but I didn't. There would be time later, after he was in custody, after she was completely safe. "I'll check on you tomorrow, okay?"

She nodded. "Okay."

I stepped out of the room and almost ran over Rick and Detective Wilson.

"I know who it is."

I told them what Dani had said, laid out my suspicions, evidence, and conclusions, and waited for their reaction.

Almost before I finished, Wilson was reaching for his cell phone. "We're going to pick him up now," he said. "It fits with the paper trail my investigators finally traced today. I think you're right. He's our man."

Now it was over.

CHAPTER
THIRTY-FIVE

Leaving Rick and Wilson to watch over Dani, I drove my dad back to Dandorff's farm to get his car, filling him in on my exchange with Wilson. I kept expecting to see a squad car pass me, red lights spinning, but I guessed the details of issuing a warrant for arrest were taking longer than I realized.

As my dad assimilated all the developments of a night that had started with birding and ended with solving a murder, he still seemed puzzled. "So who was the man passing the envelope to Olson in the casino?"

That part still bothered me. I had been sure when I saw the tape that it was Stodegard, but it had been late, and I was exhausted, and let's face it, I'd desperately wanted to pin something on the guy. Now, a day later, I wasn't convinced it had been the realtor. Yet something about the man had been so familiar to me that I could still feel the jolt of recognition. Something about the suit . . . I'd seen it somewhere.

And then I knew. It was Janssen.

Janssen was wearing the suit at the softball game. It had been overpowered by the Go Bass hat, but I was positive it was the same suit.

That also explained why the body language of the man on the video had rung a bell—I'd just seen him hours earlier, glad-handing the crowd at the game, so his style was fresh in my mind. For a split-second, I panicked: I'd given Wilson the wrong man!

Then reason reasserted itself: Janssen handing off the envelope made perfect sense. If the killer had done it himself, he'd be leaving video evidence of his guilt. This way, no one could prove he was the source of Olson's windfall, while, at the same time, he conveniently set Janssen up for the fall should Olson confess to the bribe. My guess was that Janssen didn't have a clue about the real contents of the envelope and was simply delivering it as a favor for a friend.

A friend who knew exactly where to find Olson on a late Sunday night, just like he'd known exactly where to find Nancy on a Friday evening.

A friend who was so deep into gambling debt that Detective Wilson had been stunned at the amount his investigators had finally located in loans issued to him.

A friend who realized his only way out of that debt was to sell his family land at a premium price guaranteed by the arrival of an OEI entertainment complex.

A friend by the name of Kevin Ray.

"How can you be sure it wasn't Dandorff that killed Nancy?" my dad asked as we turned down the driveway to the farmhouse. "He could have been feeding me a line tonight, covering his own tracks. It was his car that Dani saw, after all."

"That's what made everything fall into place for me, Dad. At the council meeting the other night, Dandorff mentioned that he doesn't drive at night, that Ray drives him places and likes driving his car. Since Nancy was killed in the evening, Dandorff wasn't out driving his car. Ray was."

I parked next to Dandorff's old car, noting that two other cars, besides my dad's truck, were in the farmyard. Who else was still here?

"I also realized, in retrospect, that Ray had been totally noncommittal about the proposal at the council meeting, while Janssen seemed genuinely supportive of what Karl was doing. Granted, Janssen is a politician and that alone made me not completely trust him, but the fact is, in his years on the council, he's never shown himself to be anything other than honest and up-front." I walked my dad to his pick-up. "So I guessed Janssen was the council member who attended Karl's picnic and pledged support, while Ray wouldn't commit because he wanted the deal to go through. Just now at the hospital, when Wilson told me about the loans and debts Ray had, his motive for murder was obvious. On top of that, Ray was the one who passed on the tip about Olson being approached with a bribe—a piece of information which was sure to keep the investigation focused on Dani's father and not on him."

I promised to call him tomorrow and watched him drive out to the highway. When I turned back towards the farmhouse, Bridget was on the front porch.

"Bridget, what are you still doing here?"

"Waiting for Karl to take me home. Mr. Ray wanted to show him a nest of some osprey or something near the old homestead, so he could include it in his report on the survey tonight."

"Mr. Ray?" My stomach went into free-fall.

"Yeah, he came back after everybody else left. I was keeping Grandpa company till we heard that Dani was okay. Then Mr. Ray came back and told Karl he had to see this nest so he could convince the council not to approve the deal with OEI."

Ray was here?

"There are no osprey on this land," I automatically informed her. I should know—I'd birded it enough times over the years that I could draw you a map where to find each species.

"That's weird," she said, a shade of concern clouding her face. "I thought he was acting kind of funny—Mr. Ray, I mean. Grandpa told him that he's not going to sell the farm, after all, and for a second, I thought that Mr. Ray was having a stroke because he went really, really still and his mouth fell open, but he didn't say anything, and—"

"Bridget, where's your grandpa?"

"He's inside."

"Where's Karl?"

"He's with Mr. Ray at the homestead."

I could feel the blood drain right out of my face.

"Are you okay, Mr. White? You look kind of sick."

I grabbed her arm, not exactly gently. "Bridget, do you know the way there? We've got to get there. Now."

"Sure. I know it." She looked more confused than alarmed, but even as my grip loosened a fraction in relief, I could see the beginnings of fear rising in her eyes. "Is something wrong, Mr. White? Is Karl in trouble?"

I dragged her off the porch, tearing my cell phone out of my pocket, and hit 911. "Go, Bridget!"

She set off at a run. I was right behind her.

CHAPTER THIRTY-SIX

For the second time that night, I was running hell-bent through these woods, only this time it was dark. Bridget was sprinting like she was trying to beat the ball to home plate, and I prayed she wouldn't trip. I prayed I wouldn't trip, too. I was sure there was a lot more at stake right now than a game-winning run.

Like the life of the future President of the United States.

We burst into a clearing, and I could just make out the outline of a decrepit farmhouse against the trees. I caught Bridget's arm and pulled her to a stop beside me. "Wait," I whispered, panting hard. "Let me go first."

I bolted silently up to the house, then pressed myself to the wall beside the sagging open door and listened. From inside, I could hear shuffling sounds and labored breathing. I peered around the edge of the door frame.

Enough moonlight fell through the ruined roof for me to see Ray. He had an unconscious Karl draped over his right shoulder and it looked like he was heading for an old stone fireplace on the opposite wall that was barely standing.

"Gee, Karl," Ray huffed, "you shouldn't have been looking up the flue of an old chimney. It only takes a few loose bricks to bring the whole thing down on you. You ought to keep your nose out of other people's business, too, son. It's not good for you. Too bad about that birding survey you were working on. But nobody's going to be needing it anyway."

Then, before I even knew she had come up behind me, Bridget rushed into the old house. I grabbed for her and missed. Another heartbeat and she was behind Ray, digging in, a sturdy branch in her hands.

Time slipped into slow motion. Ray started to turn toward Bridget. Bridget lifted the branch.

Paused.

Swung hard.

Swung straight.

Her follow-through was flawless.

It was the prettiest swing I'd seen all season.

If she'd been hitting a ball, it would have gone out of the park.

Touch 'em all, Bridget.

As it was, the branch connected solidly with the left side of Ray's body, sending him falling forward, Karl spilling from his shoulder. In the next instant, Bridget dropped the branch and was on her knees next to Karl. I pinned Ray down with my knee on his back and jerked his arms around into a solid hold.

"Give me your jacket, Bridget."

She ripped it off and handed it to me. Still holding Ray to the floor, I knotted the jacket roughly around his arms with one hand. He started to protest, but Bridget cut him off before I could.

"What were you doing?" she shouted at him. "Karl's hurt! He's my boyfriend!" She was ready to explode.

"He's my date for *prom*!"

"Bridget," I said, thinking I'd better distract her before she picked up another branch and went for more batting practice on Ray. "Karl's breathing, isn't he? Put your hand on his chest."

She sent one more death glare at Ray and laid her hand flat over Karl's heart. Her hand lifted and fell. "Yes. He's breathing."

"Run your fingers across his scalp. Any bleeding?"

Beneath me, Ray moaned and shifted.

Bridget dug her fingers into Karl's hair. "A little bit. Right on the back," Bridget reported, just as Karl's eyes slowly opened. "Karl! Oh,

208

Karl!" She threw her arms around his shoulders and hugged him close. "You're all right!"

I turned my attention to the man under my knee. "It's over, Ray. We got it figured out. Wilson's looking for you right now." Beneath me, I felt his body deflate, tension, or maybe the last vestiges of hope, leaking out of him like a collapsing balloon. "You shot at me the other night, didn't you? Trying to make Chris look bad."

He grunted. "The kid didn't need much help with that. He looked plenty bad to begin with."

"Convenient, right?" I asked him. "A ready-made fall guy." A wave of anger on Chris's behalf raced through my mind. Ray had deliberately used the boy. "There's only one thing I still don't understand—why did you give Nancy the gun?"

Ray said nothing.

And after this long night, knowing he'd shot at Dani, set up Chris, and killed Nancy, it made me angry.

Really angry.

Ignoring all my best instincts, all my training as a counselor, all my values as a sensitive, caring, forgiving individual, I jerked hard on his arms twisted behind his back.

He let out a howl of pain.

"Tell me," I hissed.

"She wanted a way to threaten Pete, to make him quit gambling!"

I eased up a little. "And?"

He muttered a curse. "She promised to vote for the proposal if I gave her the gun."

I could guess the next part. "She lied to you."

He didn't respond. I jerked his arms again.

"Yes! Yes, she lied. When I realized she wasn't going to vote for the deal, I told her I wanted the gun back. She refused. I knew she kept it in the car—I told her to!—so I decided to go get it myself."

"But she wasn't home."

"No. I went to the casino, Pete told me she'd gone to Chris's trailer, so I took off. I got there just as she was leaving."

I didn't want to hear the rest of it. I got off his back and looked down at him. *So this is how it ends*, I thought. I felt badly for Bridget's grandfather. His best friend was a murderer and his own property was the motive. Because of money, Nancy had been killed, Dani had been shot, Karl had been injured and Chris and his dad suspected of murder.

In the distance, I could hear sirens.

It had been a very long day.

I wanted to go home.

CHAPTER THIRTY-SEVEN

Apparently, the wish fairy was still otherwise engaged the next morning when I once again woke up to the happy repeat performance of my backyard avian choir. I stumbled out of bed, did the morning routine with minimal consciousness and drove through the Joy of Java's pickup window on my way to work. I wasn't surprised to find Rick waiting for me outside my office door.

"Morning, sunshine," he grinned.

I unlocked the door and flipped the light switch. "Please, please, tell me it really is Friday. If it's not Friday, I may have to kill myself."

"We can't have that, now, can we? You are the big, bad, bad-guy catcher. You're the talk of the station, my man." He clapped me on the shoulder. "Again."

He followed me into my office and stretched out in my visitor's chair.

"Ray came back to the farm to get the scoop on Dani," he offered, while I slid my briefcase under my desk. "He wasn't sure he'd killed her and wanted to find out if she was still a threat for him since she could identify the car he was driving when he killed Nancy. Then, when Dandorff told Ray the property deal was off, he just lost it. Went totally homicidal. He took Karl out to the homestead, planned to crush him under some fireplace bricks, then go back and shoot Dandorff and Bridget. He figured he was in so deep after shooting Nancy to guarantee the OEI deal, that it was all or nothing at that

211

point. He had to win the whole enchilada. He told Wilson the whole thing."

"How's Dani doing?"

"Good. She went home with Chris last night, but I heard that she, her dad and Chris have a meeting with a family services worker at the hospital today. It's going to take a ton of effort to try to put that family back together again, but it sounds like they're all willing to give it a chance. I hope it's the start of something good."

"You and me both."

Rick rubbed the stud in his ear. "By the way, I also heard that you got a police escort to the hospital last night."

I smiled. "Yes, I did."

"No ticket for speeding."

"That's right."

"You must have friends in the right places." He was looking smug.

I lifted an eyebrow in silent question.

Rick grinned. "I told them you were coming. After you left Dandorff's, I called the dispatcher and told them to watch for your red SUV. I figured you'd hit the pedal hard on the way to the hospital." He stood up to leave. "I also figured you could use a break. I guess I was right. Say 'thank you, Rick.'"

I laughed. "Thank you, Rick."

"If you want to give the Chat one more try, I'm available tomorrow morning."

"Sounds like a plan. Luce will want to come, too."

He paused in the doorway.

"Are you going to ask her?"

"Sure, but I know she'll want to come. She hasn't gotten a Chat in years."

Rick narrowed his eyes at me. "Not about the Chat, Bob. Are you going to take Crazy Eddie's advice and ask her to marry you? It's about time, my man."

"Hmm, let me think about this."

I looked up and considered the ceiling. "One of my best friends wants to know if I'm going to propose to my girlfriend. Said friend is a member of the local police force, which seems to maintain an inordinate amount of interest in my personal life. Do I want to tell him my plans at the risk of it becoming the talk of the station house?"

I smiled at Rick. "No, I don't."

"Aw, come on, Bob, I got you out of a ticket last night."

"And I already said 'thank you, Rick'. Now go. I have counseling to do."

"Yeah, yeah, that's what they all say." He shifted his gun holster and left.

"Mr. White."

Mr. Lenzen was in my doorway. I really didn't want to see him right now. Then again, I couldn't think of a time when I ever wanted to see Mr. Lenzen.

"Yes?" I noticed he had two students in tow. One was Collette Carsten, a pitcher on my softball team; the other was a girl I didn't know.

"These ladies have clothing violations. Would you please deal with this?"

I quickly scanned their outfits. Lots of cleavage and lots of bare thigh. Par for the course on a beautiful May morning at Savage. I stifled a sigh and covered it with a smile.

"No problem. Come on in, girls."

"Oh, and Mr. White," Mr. Lenzen added, "I wanted to thank you for adhering to the advice I gave you earlier in the week about limiting your involvement in a certain—ah—situation. I'm very pleased when my staff members keep the reputation of this school foremost in their deliberations."

"No problem," I repeated.

Obviously, he hadn't gotten the word about last night yet. Knowing the warp speed of gossip on both the student and faculty grapevines, I expected it was only a matter of minutes before he got wind of the full story. I wasn't sure if I wanted to be there or not when that happened. On the one hand, I didn't want to hear another lecture on propriety, duty, responsibility, and bond issues. On the other hand, it might be fun to see him go apoplectic. Either way, I would still come out smelling like a rose: I got the bad guy, with a little help from Bridget's stellar swing.

Okay, make that a lot of help.

Mr. Lenzen left and the girls came in, Collette dropping into a chair and the other girl leaning on the door frame.

"Coach, Bridget told us all about last night! Awesome! You guys are like—I don't know—Batman and Robin or something."

"Batman and Robin were two guys," the other girl pointed out, rolling her eyes. "How lame is that?"

Collette shot her a dirty look. "They caught a murderer," she said. "How lame is that?" she mimicked the other girl.

"Bridget was awesome, Collette," I said, making sure credit went where it belonged. "You should have seen her swing. She would have knocked it out of the park."

"But it's so romantic! She rescued Karl! How cool is that?"

Apparently pretty cool to a tenth-grade softball player.

"She is so, like, in love, Mr. White. See, that's why she could do it—her love made her strong."

The other girl snorted in disgust and rolled her eyes again. "Oh, gag."

I bit the inside of my cheek so I wouldn't burst out laughing.

"Let's get you two back in class. Have you got a jacket or shirt you can put on over your tops?"

A couple minutes later, they were on their way. I thought about Collette's remarks and smiled. Did love improve Bridget's swing? If it did, I hoped every girl on the team got a really intense case of spring fever as soon as possible.

The phone rang and I picked it up.

"Hey, Bobby. Got a minute?"

It was Lily.

"First of all, I could kill you for taking off after a murderer. What were you thinking, you idiot?"

Yup. That was my sister, all right. Ms. Sweetness and Light herself.

"You are going to give Mom and Dad heart failure at an early age if you keep this up. Secondly, the big OEI deal has now skipped town—Eric just called me—but I understand that's not your fault, so I'm not blaming you for losing the biggest business deal in my career."

"Thanks."

"Thirdly, you and Luce have to come over for dessert tonight. My place." She paused. "I have a very special surprise for you."

Something about her tone jolted me, and I felt my instincts kicking in big-time. Before I could even think twice, I knew what the surprise was: Lily was in love.

But then I realized with whom.

Eric Stodegard.

It had to be.

Somehow, the snake had slithered his way back into Lily's good graces. While I was chasing warblers and tracking down a killer, he'd been busy converting my sister's "momentary insanity" into full-blown brain loss.

This was no simple case of spring fever.

As far as I was concerned, Stodegard was a plague.

"Please, Lily," I begged, hoping against hope that I was wrong, "tell me this doesn't have to do with a certain realtor."

She laughed and said I'd just have to show up to find out. Since it was obvious she wasn't going to elaborate any further, I promised that we'd come over after Luce finished up at work about 9:30. I also needed to pick up birdseed for my feeders, so I said I'd stop by her shop on my way home from work about four o'clock.

Maybe there was still a chance I could cut Stodegard off at the pass.

Or at least prevent him from making another one at my sister.
Scum.

THE REST OF THE MORNING WAS, for a welcome change, routine. I
reviewed senior grade reports to make sure that even my most reluctant scholars were keeping on task to graduate next month. I kept
appointments with two juniors who wanted to change their class
schedules for next fall. I reminded three more girls to cover their
shoulders, cover their cleavage, cover their thighs and stay out of Mr.
Lenzen's sight. My dad called about noon, and I gave him the play-by-
play of what happened after he'd left Dandorff's farm the night
before.

"You're a good man, Bob," Dad said. "You came through for
everyone—Dani, Chris, Karl, Bridget, and Dandorff. Even Nancy
Olson. I'm proud of you."

I choked up a little and nodded even though my dad was at the
other end of a phone line and not in the room with me. It seemed that
it never made a difference what age I was—six, sixteen, twenty-four,
thirty-five—it always meant the world to me when Dad said he was
proud of me.

"You going after that Chat this weekend?"

"I am." I was relieved that he changed the subject—a guy can
only take so much emotion, and I'd gotten way more than my quota in
the past week. The chance to talk about birding, instead, was more
than welcome: it was therapy.

"If I get it, I'm just about assured of making my goal for warbler
migration. Besides the Chat, I've got just a few warblers left, but none
of them are rare. I'm pretty sure I can find them later in the month."

"I wish you'd seen Dani's face last night when I pointed the Chat
out to her and explained how you could identify it by its markings and
its call," he told me. "I don't think she ever realized you could tell
birds apart from each other. You know—the old 'you've seen one bird,

you've seen them all' bit. I told her you had to care enough to look at the details, and once you did, you never saw them the same way again."

As I hung up the phone, it dawned on me that what my dad had said about birds was just as true, if not more so, about people: you have to care enough to look at the details, and once you did, you never saw anyone the same way again. After the events of the week, I knew I saw Dani and Chris in a new light, while the aftermath of Nancy Olson's murder had revealed aspects of others I would never have guessed. Over the years, I've also come to realize it's the double-edged sword of being a school counselor who works with young people: some details about students make all the difference in enabling you to come up with the right strategy to help them manage their issues; some details you'd rather you never knew, because they broke your heart.

My bottom line, however, has never changed, no matter what the details told me: I'm in my students' corners. Before Dani, though, that had never included solving a murder.

By afternoon, details about me were flying around the school. Several of my softball players stopped by to verify that Bridget and I had nabbed a murderer, and my counseling colleagues found my account of the previous night endlessly fascinating. My instincts for self-preservation and Mr. Lenzen-avoidance were telling me that I could expect a visit from my boss as soon as the last bell rang. Instead of waiting meekly for his appearance, I decided to take a pro-active stance.

I left my office early.

Just steps away from making my escape, Alan grabbed my arm and pulled me into his empty classroom.

"Don't you ever teach?" I asked, looking around.

"My whole class is attending a scholarship presentation in the Career Center. I'm done for the day. What's your excuse?"

"Avoiding Mr. Lenzen. I figure he's got the goods on me by now, since everyone else in the building knows about last night."

"And what's he going to do? Fire the local hero? I don't think so."

"Not fire. Reprimand. At length. With eloquent language. With convoluted sentence structure. Pomp and circumstance."

"A fate worse than death."

"You got that right."

"Hold on and I'll leave with you."

He tossed some papers in his briefcase, locked his desk and his room, and we walked out into a beautiful May Friday afternoon.

"You want to go for a beer?" Alan asked as we headed out to the staff parking lot.

"Sure. I've got to stop at Lily's Landscaping first to pick up some birdseed. You want to tag along?"

"I could handle that."

I pulled out of the parking lot with Alan on my tail. For a split-second, I felt the impulse to put pedal to the metal streak down my leg, but then, just as suddenly, Rick's grin popped into my head. I let up my foot just as it touched the gas and made a slow turn onto the highway. In my rearview mirror, I could see Alan laughing.

Minutes later, we were walking through rows of tree stock in search of my sister.

"When was the last time you saw Lily? I was trying to remember on the way over here."

We turned a corner and I saw Lily setting out a tray of seedlings. Alan walked up behind her, put his arms around her waist and bent his head to kiss her on the neck.

Geez, I hadn't known Alan had a death wish. I was sure going to miss him.

"Hey!" Lily giggled. "That tickles, cowboy!"

Cowboy?

Lily giggling?

"Thanks for the save, cowboy."

Holy shit!

Bob White's *Murder on Warbler Weekend* Bird List

American Robin
Red-winged Blackbirds
Canada Goose
Yellow-rumped Warbler
Tennessee Warbler
Yellow Warbler
Black-and-white Warbler
Orange-crowned Warbler
Common Yellowthroat
Blue-winged Warbler
Eastern Wood-Pewee
Brown Thrasher
Great Crested Flycatcher
Yellow-throated Vireo
Red-eyed Vireo
Scarlet Tanager
Magnolia Warbler
Nashville Warbler
American Redstart
Hermit Thrush
American Goldfinch
House Finch
Baltimore Oriole
Northern Cardinal
Bluejay
Great Horned Owl
Rose-breasted Grosbeak

American White Pelican
Palm Warbler
Northern Parula
Pine Warbler
Ovenbird
Cerulean Warbler
Prothonotary Warbler
Louisiana Waterthrush

Acknowledgements

First and foremost, I want to thank my son Bob for sharing his birding passion, enthusiasm and knowledge with me—without him, Bob White and his friends would never have hatched in my head. Nor would the Birder Murder series exist were it not for the unfailing encouragement and love that I receive from my husband Tom and my children Rachel, Tom, Bob, Nicki and Colleen—no writer could ask for a better cheering section, or funnier repartee at the dinner table. (I still think it's a miracle no one has choked to death while laughing during meals at my home.) My thanks also go to my parents and siblings, who have believed in me as a writer since I first put pencil (or was it a crayon?) to paper.

Beyond my own nest, I owe a debt of gratitude to my North Star publisher, Corinne Dwyer, for helping me bring the Bob White Birder Murders into print and into the hands of so many wonderful readers. Her faith in this project has made all things possible. Pat Frovarp, of Once Upon A Crime in Minneapolis and bookseller extraordinaire, has kindly taken me under her wing and given me invaluable advice about the book world and marketing, which only helps me spread my own wings more widely.

As for the members of the MOU and the Audubon Society, I am privileged to have their support and interest as I continue to develop both as a writer and birder. Every time I attend an event, I just keep getting more ideas for stories and characters. Likewise, my years in educational settings inspire elements in Bob White's tales—as every writer does, I write from my own experience, although I have no problem with occasionally embellishing (or even completely altering!) the facts. Thanks, everyone.